The Grim Reader

Margaret Welch

AnniesFiction.com

Library of Congress-in-Publication Data
The Grim Reader/ by Margaret Welch
p. cm.
I. Title
                    2017933423

AnniesFiction.com
(800) 282-6643
Secrets of the Castleton Manor Library™
Series Creator: Shari Lohner
Series Editors: Jane Haertel and Janice Tate
Cover Illustrator: Jesse Reisch

10 11 12 13 14 | Printed in China | 9 8 7 6 5 4 3 2 1

"Every life has death and every light has shadow. Be content to stand in the light and let the shadow fall where it will."

—Mary Stewart

1

Faith Newberry heard the crunch of gravel as a car slowed and stopped outside her cottage. She glanced at the longcase clock in the corner of her living room and slipped a bookmark into the mystery she was reading.

"Aunt Eileen's right on time, Watson," she said to the handsome tuxedo cat curled beside her in the armchair. She put the book next to him when she got up. "Promise you won't read ahead. You know I don't like spoilers."

Watson acknowledged her joke with a blink of his green eyes. Faith slowly blinked as a sign of affection. *Dear old Watson*, she thought, stroking him between his ears. *What would we do without each other?* She took a lacy wrap from the back of the chair, draped it around her shoulders, and opened the door for her favorite aunt.

"Oh, you're wearing it," Eileen Piper said when she saw her niece. "Do a spin so I get the full effect." She'd knitted the wrap and given it to Faith as a welcome-to-Lighthouse-Bay gift.

Faith twirled, making the iridescent blue lace swirl around her. "November's put a nip in the air. Will you be warm enough?"

"We won't be out that long," Faith said, "and I don't want to cover it up."

"The way it shimmers makes it perfect for the opening of Shimmering Suspense Week."

"It *is* perfect." Faith gave her aunt a hug. "But this is *Simmering* Suspense Week, not *Shimmering*."

"They could have just called it Gloria Bauer Week. She's the real attraction. Watson isn't coming with us?"

"He has a heavy nap schedule today," Faith said. "I promised to bring him one of Brooke's shrimp puffs, though. Shall we go?" She closed the door and couldn't resist taking Eileen's arm. She loved living in the same town as her aunt, sharing a profession and their passion for books. Eileen was head librarian at the Candle House Library in Lighthouse Bay. Faith was the private librarian and archivist for the Castleton Manor literary retreat. Both women belonged to the Candle House Book Club.

Faith and Eileen skirted the Victorian flower garden, put to bed for the winter, and crossed the lawn separating the cottage from Castleton Manor. With the twilit sky for a backdrop and its lighted windows gleaming, the mansion looked almost like a chateau out of a French fairy tale. How much luckier could she be? She spent her days surrounded by a superb collection of rare books and first editions, and the former gardener's cottage on the estate came with the job. As she'd said to Watson that morning, they were living in a place where it seemed that dreams really might come true, and where a cat could nap in the lap of luxury. He seemed to agree.

Attending events like the one kicking off this evening was another perk of her job. Simmering Suspense Week had been advertised as "a celebration of the shivers running down your spine," and the manor was booked solid. Three authors were in residence for the week—Jed Knowlan, Tanya Race, and Gloria Bauer. Gloria, widely considered the reigning queen of romantic suspense, had recently received the Mary Stewart Lifetime Achievement Award. Faith was pleased that members of the Candle House Book Club had the opportunity to attend Gloria's public reading this evening.

"Have you met her yet?" Eileen asked.

"Gloria? No, but Watson and I met her dog, and Watson clearly thinks he's yappy and pretentious."

"Just as well Watson stayed home then. Do you think she brought the diamond necklace with her? The one that belonged to Mary Stewart herself? I wonder if it's too much to hope that she'll wear it tonight. By the way, I heard from Charlotte. Did you know she'll be here for the week? She's a huge fan of Gloria's."

Charlotte Jaxon, along with her sons, owned Castleton Manor. It had been Charlotte's idea—and a successful one—to turn the family estate into a destination and event center for book lovers. She lived on Martha's Vineyard now and only occasionally came back to Cape Cod.

"Marlene made sure the entire staff knows Charlotte will be here," Faith said. "She might have let the garbageman know too. I think she was trying to make sure all of us are as stressed out about it as she is."

"Poor Marlene. Charlotte doesn't bite. And if Charlotte is here, can Wolfe be far behind?"

"He said something about seeing me here this evening," Faith said, trying to sound offhand, and ignoring the twinkle in Eileen's eyes.

Wolfe Jaxon, forty-four and the eldest of Charlotte's sons, ran the family's enterprises, including the literary retreat. Between business trips, he frequently spent a week or two in private quarters on the third floor of the manor. Those stays had become somewhat more frequent since Faith's arrival, at least according to her friends in Lighthouse Bay.

The women climbed the marble stairs on the sea side of the mansion. Light from the Great Hall Gallery spilled through a dozen sets of French doors onto the tiled loggia. Inside, glasses and plates glinted in the hands of mingling guests. Faith and Eileen were about to go in when a high-pitched yip came from farther down the loggia—and then a red-brindled blur streaked toward them. He danced around their feet, yapping happily, dashed down the stairs, then bounced back up to sniff at their shoes.

"Aunt Eileen," Faith said, laughing, "meet Gloria's dog, Arfer—Sir Arfer Conan Doyle."

"Hello, sweet boy." Eileen stooped and held out her hand. The dog gave her a lick and let her rub his ears. She looked up at Faith. "There's no leash. Should he be out by himself? Do you see anyone back there, where he came from?"

"No, and you're right, he shouldn't be running loose. Let's take him in with us."

"Let me." Eileen scooped the dog into her arms. "He might get tangled in your wrap, and I seem to have had a moment of clairvoyance, because I wore the right shade of terrier for the party."

"Russet suits both of you," Faith said, "and Sir Arfer is the perfect accessory."

Marlene Russell, Faith's boss and manager of Castleton Manor, looked askance at Faith and Eileen when they entered the elegant gallery with the dog. Guests were encouraged to bring their pets with them during their stays and were offered concierge vet service and an on-site pet spa, but Marlene seemed to take every unexpected bark, yowl, or accident personally.

"Isn't he the dearest?" Eileen said to Marlene. "He calms down as soon as his feet are off the ground." The small dog's head lolled on her arm, innocent eyes gazing at the dour Marlene. "I'll go find his mama."

"Try over there by Agatha Christie." Faith nodded toward a

group gathered near the life-size statue of Dame Agatha, complete with pen in hand, at the far end of the room. They made plans to meet before Gloria Bauer's reading, and Faith watched Eileen cross the marble floor with Sir Arfer.

A waiter stopped beside Faith, handed her a napkin, and offered a tray with golden-brown phyllo triangles and stuffed mushrooms. She took a couple of each. The waiter offered the tray to Marlene. She waved him away.

"Everything is beautiful, Marlene," Faith said. "It's a lovely reception."

"The kitchen prepared the wrong appetizers."

Faith ate a mushroom and only just stopped herself from licking her fingers. But Marlene was right. Brooke Milner, the manor's sous-chef, had told Faith they'd planned special menus for the week, with each meal featuring dishes mentioned in the resident authors' books. The grand finale, at the end of the week, would be a seven-course dinner from Gloria's *Murder With a Twist of Strychnine*. Tonight's menu, taken from Tanya Race's *Sea Deep in Secrets*, should have included lobster rolls, asparagus sushi, and shrimp puffs. The mushrooms and triangles were meant for later in the week and came from Jed Knowlan's medical suspense novel *Gasping*.

"It shouldn't be a big deal to flip-flop the menus, should it?" Faith asked. "We can do Tanya's menu another day. The food is delicious. Isn't that what counts?" Faith ate one of her phyllo triangles. It was full of spinach, feta, and pine nuts. "Watson will be disappointed when I get home without shrimp puffs."

"It's not as simple as flip-flopping, and I don't care about your cat."

Watson didn't care about Marlene either, but Faith didn't see any point in hurting her feelings by saying so. "Is Brooke—?"

"Brooke is hiding in the kitchen behind her mistakes."

"I'll go mingle, Marlene. See you later." Faith almost patted Marlene's shoulder but thought better of it.

"You were giving that mushroom some serious scrutiny," said a deep voice just as Faith popped the other morsel into her mouth. "Did the poor thing offend you in some way?"

Faith looked up into Wolfe Jaxon's teasing eyes. Then she saw that Charlotte Jaxon and the author Jed Knowlan were with him. *Caught with my mouth full—what a delightful impression to make.* She chewed and swallowed. "I was playing detective, using a new form of telepathic interrogation to learn the secret of the mushroom's success." She wiped her fingers and held out her hand to Charlotte. "It's nice to see you again. We're all happy you're here."

"I wouldn't have missed this week for the world," Charlotte said. She leaned toward Faith confidentially. "I'm not ordinarily a gusher, but I'm so excited about meeting Gloria Bauer that I might not be able to help myself."

"If you want to meet Gloria," Jed Knowlan said, "she's in the middle of that scrum at the other end of the field." He raised his glass toward the guests still gathered near the Agatha Christie statue. "Probably just barely surviving. The adoration of fans can be brutal."

"Brutal? Surely you're exaggerating," Charlotte said.

"You want to see the scars of an old warrior?" Jed pretended to fumble with his top shirt button, then quit. "Nah, I'm kidding. But there's a reason writers like to sit alone in their rooms. The public part of the job doesn't always come naturally. But Tanya there," he continued, gesturing with his glass toward Tanya Race near the foot of the grand staircase, "she's part of the new social media breed. She's tough."

Tanya stood in a small group, staring up at one of the chandeliers. She was slender and willowy in a flowered dress and ruffled shrug. She struck Faith as more waifish than tough.

"She's probably wondering if you could kill someone with that chandelier," Jed said, eyeing it. "And the answer is yes. That thing is at least the size of my car."

"Are you plotting or planning?" Charlotte asked.

"You never know, but information is always useful."

"It is," Charlotte agreed. "Speaking of which, have you met Faith Newberry?"

"Faith is our resident librarian," Wolfe said. "That means watch your step, because she knows everything."

"I don't *know* everything," Faith said. "Just how to *find out* everything."

Jed shook her hand. She was surprised to feel calluses on his palm, as if he spent as much time chopping wood or digging in the dirt as he did typing. That fit his persona. Everyone else at the reception had dressed for the occasion. Jed wore a khaki shirt, cargo shorts, and hiking boots. Although the look suited him and the rough-and-tumble tone of his books, Faith had to wonder how comfortable those shorts were in New England in November. He had kind eyes, but he held her hand a few seconds longer than she thought strictly necessary.

"And what secrets did you find out during your mushroom interrogation?" he asked.

"I detected oregano and hints of mint and lemon. Am I right? The chef tried to re-create them as closely as possible."

Jed looked blank.

"You described them at the beginning of *Gasping*," Faith said. "In the Greek restaurant scene."

Wolfe laughed and clapped Jed on the shoulder. "They're ground zero for the pathogen your villain lets loose on New York City. But after three dozen books, who can blame you for being foggy on details?"

"Lost in a fog of split infinitives, broken hearts, and broken noses." Jed laughed too. "What can I say? I write what I know. But maybe I should chase down some of those mushrooms to find out just how good I am."

As the manor's librarian, Faith wasn't required to make sure that guests had all they needed at the reception, but the role came naturally to her. It also came naturally to Wolfe, and together they made their way through the room, greeting people and stopping to chat. She briefly wondered whether guests thought she and Wolfe were a couple. *Let them wonder.* Being Ms. Faith Newberry, single and independent, suited her just fine.

They were talking with Tanya when Faith saw that Gloria was finally free of her fans. Gloria stood with one hand on the Christie statue, two giants in the world of mystery and suspense. Dame Agatha looked unflappable in her marble suit and brogues. Gloria, in floor-length layered lavender silk, looked capable of flowing around the room. She wore her thick gray braid of hair wrapped around her head like a crown. And the Mary Stewart necklace—three strands of glistening round white diamonds—swirled around

Gloria's neck, meeting and forming a wave at the base of her throat. She looked absolutely royal, and there was no question that Gloria deserved her place next to Agatha Christie, the queen of mystery. But this evening, the statue definitely looked the sturdier of the two. To Faith, it almost looked like Dame Agatha had offered her arm for support and Gloria accepted it.

Then, from Gloria's left, a woman in an orange tunic and leggings raced toward Gloria like a flame touched by an accelerant. Gloria shied and turned to her right, only to see Charlotte coming at her from that side. Gloria froze between them, clearly close to panic. Faith wasn't sure that she could help, but she quickly told Wolfe and Tanya she'd see them later. She moved toward Gloria—watching as Gloria's smile wavered and faltered before she put a hand to her chest. By the time Faith reached her, Gloria's head was bent and her hand covered her eyes.

"I'm sorry," Gloria said. "I'm so sorry, but I need to go. I am—I feel ill."

"My dear, would you like me to come with you?" Charlotte asked. "Let me come with you. Shall I call a doctor?"

"No. Just . . . no, I'll be fine. Later. Or tomorrow. I . . . I have to go." And she did—almost running to get away from them and out of the Great Hall Gallery, leaving the woman in orange looking nonplussed and Charlotte mortified.

Faith glanced around. Wolfe had moved on to another group. People still talked and laughed and ate. Apparently the drama had gone mostly unnoticed. Tanya hadn't missed it though. She stared at them in a way that put an unpleasant tickle between Faith's shoulder blades. Faith turned back to Charlotte. But Charlotte had disappeared as quickly as Gloria. Marlene was there instead.

The woman in orange pointed at Faith. "It happened because Gloria saw *her* coming."

"What?" Faith asked. "What are you talking about?"

"About Gloria's reading that won't be happening," Marlene said, "because you scared her off."

The cat didn't sleep well that night. His human spent most of it tossing and turning, and that wasn't any way for a cat to get optimal slumber. He watched her from the foot of the bed, where he was safe from restless legs but lonely and cold. Finally, an hour before his human usually got up, he couldn't bear to watch her suffer anymore. Something was preying on her mind, and although he would have rather curled next to her where he would be warm, he demonstrated his selflessness by waking her with a gentle paw and insisting she get up. It was the least he could do.

Faith peered through the front window and watched the rain pounding down. Watson sat on the back of the comfy chair to her right and watched with her. Rain always seemed to interest him.

"Is this why you got me up so early?" Faith asked. "Did your whiskers feel the storm coming in?" She rubbed him between his ears and thought about how wet she was about to get. Above the pines, the sky was a lighter shade of gray. Faith decided to wait a few minutes to see if the storm would blow over.

When Faith arrived at the manor an hour later, not too terribly late, she thanked her lucky stars that Marlene was not lying in wait for her. She did, however, see the woman in orange—Alyssa Masters, according to her event name badge, which she hadn't worn the night before. Alyssa was dressed more quietly this morning, in charcoal-gray slacks and sweater, but she was no less intense. As soon as Faith stepped through the door, Alyssa grabbed her arm.

"I'm worried about Gloria," she said.

No "good morning"? No "I'm sorry I accused you of scaring the author and ruining the evening last night"? Faith looked at the hand clutching her arm, then at Alyssa's distraught face. "What's happened?"

"She didn't come down for breakfast."

"Well, that's hardly—" Faith swallowed a yawn. "I don't think the authors are required to eat every meal with the guests."

"She isn't answering the room phone or her cell." Alyssa's grip tightened. "I knocked on her door until I woke the person across the hall."

"The manor is full of out-of-the-way places and quiet corners where guests can go to be alone."

"And I've worn myself out looking in all of them."

"She might be out walking her dog," Faith said.

"Only a lunatic would go out in this kind of rain."

Faith, her trouser legs still damp, didn't argue. "Well, maybe she's in the shower. Or she turned off and unplugged so she couldn't be disturbed." *Maybe she has caller ID and she's avoiding you.* "For what it's worth, I went online last night and did some digging around. Apparently she likes her privacy—almost to the point of being a recluse."

"Then why did she agree to spend the week at a festival, surrounded by fans?"

"That's a good question, and I'm sorry I don't know the answer. Have you talked to Marlene Russell about your concern?"

At Marlene's name, Alyssa yanked her hand from Faith's arm as if she'd been stung. Faith felt her pain—she'd been stung by Marlene a few times herself. At last night's reception, for instance, and then all night long in her dreams.

"I'll see what I can find out for you, Alyssa. You're kind to be concerned." *Kind or a fanatic. Either way, how could it hurt to go check on our star author?*

2

Faith ran lightly up the grand staircase to the second floor. Gloria had been given the du Maurier Suite—a large corner bedroom with windows facing the woods on one side and the sea on the other, and a book-filled sitting room with a fireplace. The private bath had a deep spa tub, perfect for relaxing. Faith could picture the reclusive Gloria taking her meals in the suite and happily holing up there for the entire week. If she were Gloria, Faith would certainly be tempted to do that.

As she drew near the suite, the door opened. A young woman in the manor's housekeeping uniform backed out of the room and, without looking in Faith's direction, pulled the door closed.

"Good morning," Faith said.

Startled, the young woman dropped what she had in her hand.

"Sorry, I didn't mean to sneak up on you," Faith said. "You're Lindsey, aren't you? I guess you are, unless you're wearing someone else's name tag." Faith smiled, expecting the small joke to raise at least half a smile from Lindsey. She couldn't tell if it did. Lindsey had stooped for the things she'd dropped—keys and a pale lavender envelope. "Do you know if Gloria's having breakfast in her suite this morning?" Faith asked.

"No."

"Do you mean—" Faith stopped short when she caught sight of the name handwritten on the envelope Lindsey had scooped up—*Charlotte Jaxon*. A personal note from Gloria? Faith felt sure Charlotte would appreciate that after the scene at the reception. But Lindsey was already moving away down the hall. "Wait, did you mean no, she isn't having breakfast in her suite, or no, you don't know?"

Lindsey said something, but Faith didn't catch it.

She watched the young woman disappear around the corner. Then, with a shrug, she knocked on Gloria's door. Hearing nothing, she knocked again and called Gloria's name. Still no response. No answering creak of a floorboard or bedsprings and no sound of a running shower or a tub being filled. No *arf* from Sir Arfer. If Alyssa hadn't told her that she'd knocked and tried phoning Gloria, and if Faith hadn't just seen Lindsey come out of the room, she might have thought Gloria was an extremely sound sleeper. Perhaps she and Sir Arfer had gone out in the rain after all. Or driven into Lighthouse Bay for breakfast.

Faith tried the doorknob. It turned. She knew Marlene would have her head for entering a guest's room, but she couldn't ignore a sudden tingle of concern. Knocking and calling Gloria's name again, she opened the door.

The curtains were closed and only the light spilling in from the hall let Faith see she was in the sitting room. She stayed with her hand on the doorknob, listening as she oriented herself—fireplace to her left, windows and what must be a view of the sea ahead, a wall of bookshelves on her right, door to the bedroom immediately to her right. The bedroom door was open. That room was darker than the sitting room.

"Gloria?" Faith called softly this time. She didn't hear the regular breathing of someone asleep, and by now she was convinced Gloria wasn't in the suite. Illogical though it might be, calling her name made Faith feel less like she was intruding.

She found a light switch on the wall near the door and flipped it. A floor lamp near the desk came on, showing her walls the color of butterscotch, flowered slipcovers on chairs, a love seat, and a desk that would be a perfect place to set up a laptop. Again, it was easy to imagine Gloria deciding to spend all her time, or all her spare time anyway, in the suite, especially on a rain-drenched morning. So where was she? And what was it about the sitting room that bothered Faith? Or was it just that she'd caught Alyssa's bug for melodrama?

Faith stepped into the bedroom, feeling for a light switch on the wall. When she found it, a lamp on a small table just inside the door to her left came on. Its pool of light gave her only a hint at the size of the room. It did show her a floor lamp between a desk and a wardrobe on her left though. She turned it on as well.

Heavy damask drapes shrouded six floor-to-ceiling windows. It made sense that Gloria had closed the drapes before going to bed in case the eastern light streamed in earlier than she wanted to rise. But those windows formed the corner of the room with their coveted views of the sea and woods. Even on a gray day like today the views were spectacular. Why hadn't she opened the curtains this morning to drink it all in?

A chaise and a couple of upholstered chairs faced the seaward windows. The windows facing the woods shared a wall with another fireplace and an antique secretary desk with pigeonholes and drawers. A framed photograph hung above the secretary desk. In it a young Daphne du Maurier, typing at a nearly identical desk, turned to look over her shoulder at the camera.

The colors in this room were forest green and deep raspberry; the woodwork, polished cherry. Except for the half tester bed with its ornately carved head against the wall to Faith's left, a visitor might almost forget it was a bedroom.

The base of the lamp Faith turned on was in the shape of a charming but startled-looking shorebird. The bird was staring at the bed, and when Faith followed its gaze to the bed, she decided she couldn't blame the bird for being surprised. She imagined it had the same question running through its head that she had running through hers. What had Lindsey been doing in Gloria's suite? She hadn't brought or taken away tea or a breakfast tray. And she definitely hadn't been there to make the bed. Judging by the rumpled and twisted sheets and the duvet spilling off onto the floor, Gloria's night had been even more restless than Faith's.

A second lamp, with another shorebird, sat on a table beside the bed. It appeared to be the mate of the first, but this bird was all action. With its neck outstretched, it looked like it was running for dear life. Faith couldn't help thinking the bird might have the right idea. Still, she decided to be thorough—thoroughly nosy, perhaps, but if something wasn't quite right, she'd need to risk getting in trouble by making a report to Marlene. And in that case, thorough was the way to go.

The bathroom door, slightly ajar, was in the far corner of the room, beyond the wardrobe. She started toward it, realized she was tiptoeing, and made herself walk normally. When she reached the door, she fought the temptation to peek around the edge of it first. Instead she tapped on it and went in.

Faith didn't know what she'd been worried about. It was just a bathroom. Although it really wasn't *just* a bathroom. It was larger and more luxurious than most hotel bathrooms. Even if the comfort of the suite or the views didn't impress Gloria, Faith was sure this bathroom would.

The scent of lavender lingered in the air. One of the manor's fluffy white bath towels hung over the side of the tub, with a wrung-out washcloth beside it. Another damp washcloth lay on the counter. The bath mat was on the floor, the thick pile flattened where wet feet had been. *Just a bathroom with nothing to tell. And yet . . .*

As a courtesy, the manor supplied a range of toiletries for guests. They were products made in Lighthouse Bay, scented with almond and vanilla. But Faith smelled lavender, and the jars and bottles of almond and vanilla were still arranged in a basket on the counter, so Gloria must have used her own toiletries. Faith looked at the counter, then at the bath, into the shower, and behind the door. There weren't any of Gloria's personal items in the bathroom. And then she realized she hadn't seen any personal items in the bedroom either. She went back to double-check.

No nightgown or robe on the bed. No book on the nightstand. No sweater on the back of a chair. No electronics, spare cords, pen, paper, or notebook on the desk. Feeling more and more uneasy, Faith opened the drawers and found nothing beyond Castleton Manor stationery and tourist brochures. Then she looked in the wardrobe and found only empty hangers. And when she ran back to the sitting room, she realized that was what had bothered her there as well. There wasn't a slipper, suitcase, toothbrush, or dog bowl to be found anywhere. Except for the disturbed bed, the damp washcloths and towel, and the footprints on the bath mat, Gloria and Sir Arfer might never have been in the suite.

What a shame. The guests would be so disappointed. People might even leave, and she couldn't blame them.

She heard a noise in the hall and went to the door. *Did someone just slip around the corner? Was someone watching me?* She scolded herself for being paranoid and went back to close the wardrobe door she'd left hanging open.

"Watson!" In her surprise at seeing her cat, her voice came out as a squeak. That didn't disturb him. He stood with his front paws on the wardrobe's sill, leaning forward and sniffing the air inside, his whiskers alert. Faith scooped him up. "Come on, old boy." She closed the wardrobe door. "Your talent for getting into places where you don't belong might give me a heart attack someday," she said, carrying Watson to the suite's door. "There's no mystery here though. The lady has vanished, but no game is afoot. I'm very much afraid we've scared the poor woman away."

Watson gave a plaintive mew as Faith pulled the suite door closed behind them.

She couldn't agree more. Now she'd have to break the news to Marlene. And even worse, to Charlotte.

Faith checked first to see if it was still raining before letting Watson out one of the French doors onto the loggia. But the sky was clearing, and she was sure he'd be happier in a puddle of sunshine outside than he would be if she took him with her to find Marlene. He and Marlene seemed to have reached a balance in their relationship—they disliked each other equally.

Faith first looked for Marlene in the breakfast room. Her nose encouraged her to sit down with the guests still enjoying Brooke's coffee and cinnamon rolls, but she didn't let her nose or Brooke's rolls lead her astray. Employees were not allowed to eat with the guests except by special invitation. Marlene wasn't there anyway. Neither was Gloria, although Faith would have been completely surprised to find the author hobnobbing with the guests. Alyssa *was* there and Faith moved on to the gift shop before Alyssa saw her. She knew that Marlene made a habit of stopping in the gift shop each morning, where she critiqued and made minor changes to the displays, much to the annoyance of Iris Alden, who managed the shop. When Faith looked in, Iris was starting to wrap one of the hand-painted bisque replicas of Castleton Manor that were exclusive to the shop.

"You sold one," Faith said. "How nice."

"To a guest from last week who was sorry to get home without it," Iris said. "I love it when that happens, and it would scare me to mail them if I didn't actually know a thing or two about wrapping ceramic objects safely." Iris was a retired museum conservator who had specialized in caring for Early American decorative art. She and her husband, a former professor of German literature, had retired to Lighthouse Bay several years earlier. But as Iris told Faith, she couldn't stay retired.

"Have you seen Marlene this morning?" Faith asked.

"She came in and instructed me in the finer points of wrapping." Iris pointed at a mug sitting on the sales counter. "When I'm finished with this package—my way—I'll enjoy my a.m. coffee. And by 'a.m.,' I mean 'after Marlene.'"

Faith laughed. "Everything looks just right, Iris, as always. I'll check her office, but if you see her again, will you ask her if I've given her the news about Gloria? And if I haven't found her yet, that question should bring her running to find me."

"What news?"

"I'd better tell Marlene first."

"Understood, though inquiring minds want to know."

"And they will soon enough. Thanks, Iris."

Marlene's office was one of several in the basement along a corridor of rooms that had been servants' quarters in an earlier era. To make up for their humble beginnings, each office had been created out of two of the original rooms with the connecting wall removed. Marlene's office was especially appealing. It was painted a delicate peach and had a wallpaper border running around the room up near the ceiling. The border was a reproduction of a floral pattern that had been used a century ago in some of the bedrooms that were now part of the Jaxon family's private quarters on the third floor.

Unfortunately for Faith, approaching Marlene in her pretty surroundings didn't make her any easier to deal with. She found Marlene at her desk in the office and told her what she'd found—or not found—in Gloria's suite.

"But she signed a contract," Marlene said. "You do know that, don't you?" She'd stared at Faith throughout her report, not moving. Faith wasn't sure she'd even blinked. Now Marlene inched a sheet of paper a fraction to the left on the blotter in front of her, putting the paper more exactly in the center. Then she looked at Faith again, one eye narrowed. "I find it hard to understand how she can be so disrespectful. Or negligent. It was a *contract*. And you can bet I'll be getting that contract out and reading it with a fine-tooth comb to see what recourse we have and what steps to take. And just you see if *I* ever buy another one of her books or ask her to sign the ones I already own."

"Well, when it comes down to it," Faith said, trying to reason, although reasoning with Marlene rarely worked, "we don't know for *certain* that she's gone. Or that she's gone for good."

"But isn't that what you just told me? That she's cleared out? Without notice? And didn't she leave the reception early last night, after a confrontation with *you*?" Marlene's emphasis made it clear she thought Faith was responsible for part or all of this fiasco.

"That isn't what happened last night." Faith was still standing in front of Marlene's desk. Marlene hadn't invited her to sit, and Faith was glad she hadn't. Looking down at her gave Faith a bit of an edge. Over the past few months, she'd learned to look for those edges when she had to confront Marlene. She'd also learned how effective it was to speak clearly and firmly to the exasperating woman. Returning Marlene's icy stare helped too, and she did that now. "And in fact, I just realized she might have left a note for Charlotte."

News of the note popped Marlene's eyes open wide. "A note? Where is it? Didn't you think that might be an important detail? I was under the impression librarians prided themselves on being detail oriented. Why didn't you tell me?"

"I just did." Faith's terse answer appeared to irritate Marlene more than she already was. And whether it was the answer or the irritation that distracted her, Faith didn't care. She was happy the distraction kept Marlene from asking any more questions about the note. "If you'd like, Marlene, I'll go talk to Charlotte and find out if she's heard from Gloria and knows what's going on. Maybe it isn't as bad as you think."

"As bad as *I* think? You mean as bad as *you'd* better realize this is. And no. You don't need to go bothering Charlotte. I'll talk to her. I cannot fathom why Charlotte didn't contact me immediately if there's been any communication from Gloria. Especially if it's something that affects this week's programming. Now get back to the library and figure out how to fill the holes Gloria blew into our program schedule when she ran away."

Faith had an hour to solve the problem before the first program was due to start. "I'll be in the library, then," she said. "Let me know if you hear anything, will you please?"

Marlene gave no sign she'd heard the request. She was already on the phone, acting as if Faith were long gone or had never been there.

Faith didn't snap a salute. Marlene's attitude called for it, and she might actually enjoy it if she noticed. Faith knew Marlene was right, though. They had an enormous manor full of guests who'd paid plenty for the privilege of listening to, learning from, and hobnobbing with three star authors, not two. Gloria's desertion meant Faith's work was cut out for her, and she'd better get started. She left the corridor of offices, ruminating on a question as she ran back up to the first floor to her place of inspiration and refuge—the library.

Where was Gloria Bauer?

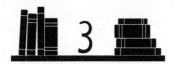

3

The guest library was Faith's primary reason for being at Castleton Manor. The library managed to be both magnificent and cozy at the same time, and Faith—along with most of the guests at the manor—considered it to be the crowning jewel of the estate. Every square foot of the library was designed to focus attention on the amazing collection of books resting on shelves rising two stories to the frescoed ceiling above. From the massive fireplace—large enough to roast an ox—to the warmth of the walnut paneling to the garnet red of the draperies, chairs, and padded benches, all the furnishings and appointments had been chosen to invite and then pamper serious scholars and casual readers alike.

Faith entered the library, slowing her feet at the same time as she consciously slowed and deepened her breathing. She immediately felt calmer. Being surrounded by books always did that for her, and even Marlene on a rampage couldn't change that.

She walked into the middle of the room and turned in a circle, scanning the second-floor balcony as she listened for the telltale rustle of a reader turning pages. Some of the manor guests spent most of their time in the library, staking out a favorite niche or chair and hardly budging except for meals. A few even took their meals in the library and stayed late each night under the glow of a reading lamp. Faith understood that kind of devotion to books and literature. She would just as soon be alone this morning, though, and was happy when she didn't find anyone already there.

In the weeks leading up to Simmering Suspense Week, she'd

read as many novels, short stories, and articles by Gloria Bauer, Jed Knowlan, and Tanya Race as she could. The plan had been for her to introduce this morning's informal author chat, moderate several panel discussions among the three authors, and interview each of them individually on different days throughout the week. She'd exchanged e-mails with them, asking questions and getting their input, and she felt thoroughly prepared and ready for those events. But now, without Gloria . . .

No, she would not panic. She was in the perfect place to steady her nerves for the juggling act that lay ahead. She could figure this out. She would—

Something rubbed against her ankles. "Eep!" Too late to keep herself from shrieking, Faith slapped a hand to her mouth. Then she lowered it and apologized to Watson. She stooped to rub between his ears. "I'm so sorry, sweetie pie. If you like, we can blame it on Marlene. She could even make a high tension wire feel tense."

With a purr, Watson turned his head so she could scratch his jaw and chin.

"There, that's better, isn't it? Who let you back in?"

Watson purred more loudly and leaned in for more.

"Not telling?" Faith said. "That's okay. Cats are allowed to keep secrets."

Watson ended his purr on a high note and then, his stub of a tail held high, walked toward a pair of wingback chairs. The chairs faced French windows looking out onto the front terrace.

"It might be easier to work at the desk," Faith called after him. "I'll let you bat a few paper clips around."

Watson stopped and looked over his shoulder at her, then hopped up into one of the wingbacks and settled himself.

"The chairs it is."

Faith didn't have an office like Marlene's, and she did occasionally wish she could count on being able to work in private without having to retreat to her cottage. On the other hand, she could think of the whole library as her office, and what she called her "desk" was the most amazing piece of antique library furniture she'd ever seen—an ornately carved walnut table that was a Jaxon family heirloom.

Faith retrieved a blank notebook from the desk and went to join Watson. She slipped off her shoes and tucked her feet under her in one of the tall wingbacks. Watson abandoned his chair to nestle in her lap, then tipped back his head to give her a slow blink. She leaned down and touched her nose to his.

"This is perfect," she said. "You purr and I'll think." She settled her head into the wing of the chair, then realized how dangerously comfortable that was. "But don't let me fall asleep." Watson stretched out a paw and rested it on her arm. "I knew I could count on you."

Faith opened the book to a fresh page and jotted the main points of the day's program schedule: the chat with all three authors—now two—due to start at ten, and the first of the interviews at two that afternoon. Luckily the first interview was with Tanya Race. Faith had the schedule and all her files of notes in the tablet tucked inside the portfolio in her bag, but brainstorming called for falling back on an old habit—doodling.

A series of spirals grew on the page as she considered how Gloria's absence would affect the chat and the panels. Guests would be disappointed, that was a given. But what about the other authors? Tanya and Jed might not mind basking in more of the limelight this morning than originally planned. So the simplest solution would be to go ahead without Gloria.

Watson opened one eye and looked at her.

"I know. Easier said than done," Faith said to him. It could work though. She had copious notes from her preparation reading. And Gloria's interview wasn't until Thursday. With luck, Gloria would be over her case of nerves by then and back at the manor where she belonged. And if not . . .

Smaller spirals and rows of spikes sprouted from the large spirals as Faith mulled over Gloria not coming back. If she didn't return, Faith could probably pull together enough material to lead a discussion *about* Gloria in place of the interview *with* her. It could be a discussion of the evolving themes in her books over the decades she'd been writing. And if any guests were so unhappy about Gloria's absence that they felt the need to complain, then that's what Marlene was for.

As Faith wrote down her new plans in the notebook, she heard the soft steps of someone entering the library. New guests often had questions about the collection and borrowing privileges, so she added a quick note about looking for reviews of Gloria's earlier books, and then she started to shift Watson so she could get up to greet the visitor.

Watson stopped her. His paw still rested on her arm and he gently but insistently extended his claws and looked at her as if to say, "Wait and listen."

Faith was about to scold him when she heard someone else enter, a young woman by the sound of her voice.

"Excuse me, Mrs. Jaxon?" the young woman said.

"Yes?"

"This came for you."

"Thank you, Lindsey. May I bother you for a cup of tea?"

Faith didn't hear an answer right away and wondered if Lindsey had only nodded. Maybe she was terribly shy. Then she heard the young woman say, "Of course. It's no bother. I'll be right back."

One set of footsteps receded. Another approached Faith's desk, and then Faith realized three things all at once. First, Watson's claws seemed more insistent than ever that she stay in the chair. Second, from the sound of drawers opening and shutting and the pencils in her cup being stirred, Charlotte was looking for something. Then, judging from the distinct sound of paper being slit, she'd found the letter opener and used it. Third, it was too late now, and it would be much too awkward, for her to let Charlotte know she was there, so close yet hidden from view. Faith shrank back into her chair and was rewarded with an approving gaze from Watson. Still, she felt guilty. Even more so when Charlotte started talking to herself.

"Of all the silly, melodramatic nonsense. If you have cold feet or if you're so antisocial, Gloria, then just say so in the first place, before we advertised that you'd be here and had people sign up to meet you. This is beyond ridiculous."

Faith heard an angry crumple of paper and something hit the bottom of the wastepaper basket. She glanced at her watch. She still had plenty of time before the author chat, but what if Lindsey brought an entire pot of tea and Charlotte stayed in the library to drink it? *Did that possibility occur to you?* she thought, while trying to catch Watson's eye. Watson's attention was applied to washing his right ear. Was he avoiding her? She couldn't tell, but he abruptly stopped washing when they heard someone else come in.

"Oh, the tea," Charlotte said, sounding exasperated. "I've changed my mind. I'm sorry, Lindsey."

Again, footsteps receded. They must have been Charlotte's because Faith heard Lindsey mutter, "Yeah, well, that's nice for you. I wish I was so lucky that I could change mine."

Faith really felt like an eavesdropper at that point. Charlotte hadn't been unkind to Lindsey and didn't deserve Lindsey's sour remarks and attitude—an attitude that could easily get her fired. Faith was glad when she heard Lindsey leave. Watson might have been glad, but she couldn't tell. He jumped down from her lap and stretched. "You're as guilty as I am," she told him. He didn't seem bothered by that. He sauntered off, and Faith went over her introductory notes for the chat.

Guilt was a useless emotion, and the cat never let it disturb his dignity or sense of well-being. Early in his relationship with his human, after an incident involving a bowl of cereal and some fresh, creamy milk, he'd tried sharing his insights on guilt with her. She hadn't caught on. But he was fond of her and patient, so he would continue his attempts to get his viewpoint across. Just now he'd waited until he was sure he'd caught her eye. Then he'd turned his back on her and casually walked away, illustrating the concept of Stepping Away From The Guilt.

But curiosity—that was another story. That was an emotion he could get behind. Or beside. Or on top of, inside, or underneath. Curiosity was a guiding principle in his life, and right this moment it was guiding him to the wastebasket under Faith's desk. He'd heard one of the intruding females drop something in it. Something that made an intriguing, crinkly, rustling noise. Ever prudent, he sniffed the wastebasket first. Then he looked over the rim. Then he tipped it over.

"What are you up to over there, Rumpy?" Faith called. Rumpy was her favorite nickname for Watson, especially when he was being silly and clumsy. His stubby tail sometimes made him less than graceful, and rather than insult him by laughing, she'd come up with the name Rumpy.

Watson came into view playing kitty soccer with a crumpled ball of paper. Faith did laugh at that.

"You funny thing. Are you going to try for a goal?"

Watson batted the ball of paper under her chair.

"Score! You are truly a talented athlete, Watson, but we can't leave that there." She retrieved it and then looked from it to him. The paper was pale lavender. He sat erect, gazing at her. Faith thought of that unblinking gaze as his serious look, and it always made her think he was trying to tell her something.

She leaned around the edge of the wingback chair, saw the overturned wastepaper basket under her desk, and straightened back up. If the ball of lavender paper had been in that wastepaper basket, then it had been discarded. And if it had been discarded, then it no longer belonged to anyone, much less Charlotte Jaxon. She glanced at Watson. He continued to stare at her.

Despite her rationalizing, Faith couldn't help feeling a fresh twinge of guilt. But if this was a letter from Gloria, it might shed light on her state of mind or her plans, which directly affected Faith. And judging by Charlotte's reaction to it, the note didn't contain good news. Faith carefully opened the scrunched paper, then smoothed it out on her lap. She froze. What she found herself staring at wasn't a note from Gloria.

I have Gloria Bauer. She is safe. For now. But she will only remain that way if you follow my instructions. Do not go to the police. Do not tell anyone. Do not try to find her. To get her back, deliver the Stewart necklace by midnight Wednesday. Leave it at the public library in hold box 3, using access code 1004. Follow these instructions exactly. If you fail to do this, Gloria will not live to write another word. You are being watched.

4

Faith had never seen a real ransom note before. If it was real. And if it was real, her fingerprints and Charlotte's were all over it, and she might have destroyed others when she smoothed it out, though the kidnapper might have been smart enough to wear gloves.

The note still lay on her lap, but at some point she'd pulled her hands away from it, as if its threats pricked her fingers. She reread the ugly, choppy, typed sentences, trying to understand how Charlotte had been so sure the threats weren't real.

If you fail to do this, Gloria will not live to write another word. You are being watched.

The last two sentences were the heart-stoppers. Faith couldn't see anything about them or the rest of the note that would make Charlotte think this wasn't real. And if it was . . . The possibility splintered her calm. She felt her thoughts race off in all directions, tripping over more worries than she could count as they ran. *The note is lavender, like the envelope Lindsey dropped outside Gloria's suite. Was this note in that envelope?* It might have been. But if Charlotte was right and it was melodramatic nonsense, then who would play such a cruel and tasteless joke? Charlotte seemed to think Gloria had sent the note herself. But why would Gloria do that?

And then there was the demand for the Mary Stewart necklace. Gloria had worn it the night before. It must be worth—Faith didn't even like to think how much that beautiful, glittering mass of diamonds was worth. Obviously the kidnapper, if there was a kidnapper, hadn't gotten the necklace when he'd snatched Gloria. Had she entrusted it to the manor's safe?

"Rumpy," Faith said to Watson. Even to herself, her voice sounded tight and unnatural. She stopped and put a hand on top of her head and left it there for a slow count of ten. It was a simple trick she'd learned for dealing with stress in her job as a librarian and archivist at the university back in Boston. There'd been a lot about her life in Boston that was stressful, and a calm hand on her head helped her feel like her brains weren't about to fly up and out.

"Okay," she said, testing her vocal cords when her slow count reached ten. She was back in control of voice and mind. "I have the horrible feeling that this note isn't nonsense."

Faith got up, and Watson followed her to the middle of the room. She looked through different eyes now—at the second-floor balcony, the fireplace, into the corners. The manor had any number of secret passages between rooms and floors. According to Wolfe, some were so well hidden that even he wasn't sure they'd all been found. Some, no doubt, were perfect for spying, as the kidnapper claimed to be doing. She turned in a full circle, wondering who it could be. A guest or one of the other authors? And then another terrible idea occurred to her. What if Charlotte's reaction to the note had already sealed Gloria's fate?

Watson, facing the door and crouched on his haunches, growled low in his throat. Faith whirled around. No one was there. But were those footsteps disappearing down the hall? She ran to the door. The hall was empty, but she heard the soft click of a door being closed. This was so much like what had happened when she was in Gloria's suite. But the manor was huge and full of hallways and doors and dozens of people moving around all day.

She turned toward Watson. "This is beginning to feel like a plot from one of Gloria's own books."

Ah, books. Faith often found answers within their pages or while surrounded by their calming influence. She glanced around the library again and knew what to do. She'd work around Gloria's absence this morning, as planned. If possible, she'd keep an eye on Charlotte and an eye out for anyone who might be watching Charlotte.

And she'd call a special meeting of her trusted friends in the Candle House Book Club. They'd helped her untangle previous mysteries, and she was confident they would offer good advice. But first she would call Aunt Eileen and ask her to convince Charlotte to attend the meeting that afternoon. She walked outside and dialed her aunt.

"And you can't tell me what this is about?" Eileen asked after hearing Faith's carefully worded request. "Charlotte and I are old friends, but it would be easier if I could give her at least some idea."

"Mmm, no."

"Why do you sound like you're shivering?"

"I'm out on the lawn and didn't put on my jacket." *The better not to be overheard by spies and kidnappers*, Faith added, but only in her head. She could have stayed inside and sent Eileen a text to avoid being overheard, but she thought the request was complicated enough to warrant a call. And she wanted to hear her aunt's reassuring voice.

"Intrigue is all well and good for the rest of us," Eileen said, "but Charlotte likes details and doesn't put up with nonsense."

"Tell me about it. You can tell her it's a surprise for Simmering Suspense Week."

"A surprise that I can't tell her over the phone?"

"If Charlotte shows up at the meeting, Aunt Eileen, I owe

you dinner at the restaurant of your choice. And dessert."

Faith didn't see Watson when she went back inside. She called him, but he'd pulled one of his disappearing acts and didn't answer or show his whiskers. *Is that what Gloria did?* She looked at the ransom note again. Maybe Charlotte was right and the note was nothing but nonsense, the latest piece of fiction from the reigning queen of romantic suspense. But what if Charlotte was wrong, and in her disbelief, she told someone about the ransom note? And what if the kidnapper found out?

There were too many what-ifs in this situation for Faith's liking. She put the lavender note into her pocket and tucked the doodled-in notebook into her portfolio with her tablet. The author chat was taking place in the Great Hall, adjacent to the gallery where the reception had been the night before. *But wouldn't it be great to peek into the gallery and see Gloria standing by the Agatha Christie statue, surrounded by a group of adoring fans like she was last night?* Faith's wish was nice, but it went ungranted. Dame Agatha stood alone.

A portable stage was set up at one end of the Great Hall. Arcs of chairs faced the stage with three burgundy leather armchairs arranged in a conversation group in the center. Potted palms on either side of the group of chairs gave the arrangement the look of an old-fashioned men's club.

Guests arrived, some milling and some claiming seats. Faith had a brief moment of concern when she didn't see Tanya or Jed, but then she caught sight of them in conversation near the grand staircase. Jed had called Tanya tough the night before, and Faith could see that in her posture. As she watched, Tanya appeared to be listening to Jed, and then she made a slashing motion with one hand. Jed pulled back. Then he laughed and walked away. Marlene arrived at that moment and stole Faith's attention away from the authors. The manager stopped to stare at the stage, then marched over to stand next to Faith.

"They were supposed to use the ferns as decor for the author chat."

"Hello, Marlene," Faith said without turning to look at her. "The palms are fine."

"The palms are for the interviews. The ferns are for the chat."

"They look really good up there, but if you're worried, it should be easy enough to get them switched."

"With people already sitting down? No. On top of everything else that's going wrong, that would be incredibly tacky."

Now Faith did turn to Marlene. "What else has happened?" She put her hand on her pocket. The note was still there, safe, although in her imagination it suddenly weighed her pocket down like a sheet of lead.

"Shh. Not so loud. I'm talking about Gloria defecting. What are you going to say when you introduce the chat? We don't want it to become general knowledge. We need to cover for her. Maybe I should . . ." Marlene's voice trailed off unhappily.

"It's okay. I can do it, Marlene." Faith knew Marlene didn't enjoy speaking in front of groups. Brief welcomes and standard announcements were about all she could handle without breaking into a sweat. "Why don't you tell me what you'd like me to say? Will that work?"

Marlene nodded, which was about as close as Faith ever saw her come to offering a compliment or a pat on the back.

"By the way, did you get a chance to tell Charlotte about Gloria?"

"A chance?" Marlene asked. "It wasn't chance at all. I said I would tell her and I did."

"When?"

"Right after you told me Gloria left, as if it's any of your business."

"Sorry, I didn't mean to be nosy," Faith said. "I only wondered what Charlotte said when you did tell her, or if you've seen her since."

"Mrs. Jaxon is not at our beck and call."

"I realize that, but—"

"And if she said anything," Marlene continued on top of Faith, "I don't see how it's any of your business. Furthermore, you are not to disturb her."

Faith swallowed her irritation at Marlene and her "furthermores." "Tell me what you want me to say about Gloria. Then I'd better get this author chat started."

"Tell them the truth. That she's been called away but hopes to be with us again soon."

"What?" Faith felt a surge of hope. It would be just like Marlene to hold back vital information until the last minute. "You mean you've heard from Gloria?"

"No. I'm merely asking you to do what all our authors do—create a fiction and make it sound like some version of the truth."

Faith held her tongue as she watched Marlene stalk away. Then she joined Tanya near the stage. Jed joined them and they were each fitted with a lapel mic. Before the mics were turned on and tested, Faith told them about the change in plans.

"Called away?" Jed asked. Faith wasn't sure whether he sounded confused or suspicious.

"Wherever she's gone," Tanya said, "she's left us a gift and we should enjoy it while we can. You know as well as I do that as soon as she's back we'll be invisible again."

The look Jed gave Tanya made her take a step back.

"Okay, maybe *you* won't be invisible," she amended. "I didn't mean that as criticism of Gloria, anyway. She's earned center stage, and I'll enjoy sitting in her shadow when she's back. But for now, I'm grabbing some sunshine."

"Go for it." Jed waved Tanya to the stage steps with an exaggerated flourish.

Faith followed them up the steps, hoping they'd play nice during their chat. The buzz of anticipation in the room increased when Tanya stepped to the center of the stage and curtsied. The buzz turned to delighted laughter and applause when Jed curtsied beside her. Faith stood to the side, glancing over the audience while the laughter died down. Most of the seats were full. Alyssa had claimed one in the front row. Halfway back, Faith saw Midge Foster, Castleton Manor's concierge vet and a member of the Candle House Book Club. Always friendly, Midge waved.

Faith waved back and took that as her cue to get started. She walked to the front of the stage and called, "Good morning!"

Most of the audience echoed her greeting, sounding like a group of unusually eager and well-trained schoolchildren, which made Faith laugh.

"Welcome to our first full day of Simmering Suspense Week. I'm Faith Newberry, the librarian here at Castleton Manor. Did you all receive the program brochure?"

Heads nodded.

"Excellent. We have a wide variety of events planned for you, starting with this morning's informal author chat and finishing out the week with a banquet honoring Gloria Bauer and her Mary Stewart Lifetime Achievement Award. At two o'clock this afternoon, for anyone interested, I'll be giving a tour of Castleton

Manor's library. And of course, to keep you in an appropriate state of suspense throughout the week, we've planned a few surprises for you along the way. Now it's my pleasure—"

Before Faith could utter another word, Alyssa was on her feet, waving her program guide over her head. As everyone stared at her, the young woman shouted, "I demand to know what you're doing to get Gloria Bauer back!"

F aith looked quickly at Charlotte to gauge her reaction to Alyssa's outburst. A narrowing of her eyes? An indrawn breath? But Charlotte sat too far away to tell. Charlotte was staring at Alyssa, but so was everyone else. Everyone except Marlene. She was conveniently absent.

"Well?" Alyssa crossed her arms, knocking her glasses askew with the brochure as she did so.

Faith hoped she looked cool, calm, and in control—the opposite of how she felt. She took a step closer to the edge of the stage and tried smiling at Alyssa to defuse her rage. Loud, enthusiastic clapping came from behind her. *Now what?*

"That," Jed said, "is the best introduction to the topic of suspense it has ever been my pleasure to witness. What's your name?" He leaned toward Alyssa. He looked and sounded completely sincere.

Flustered, Alyssa looked around, then stammered, "A-Alyssa Masters."

"Well, Alyssa Masters, that was *masterful*. Don't you think so, Tanya?"

"Absolutely," Tanya immediately agreed. "All the elements were there—surprise, a hint of danger or sinister intent, worry, a questionable outcome. Absolutely top-notch."

"And Faith did a great job of foreshadowing with her comment about 'surprises to come,'" Jed added. "Thank you, ladies, for getting our chat off to the perfect start." He applauded again and the audience joined in.

Alyssa, obviously confused but proud of her contribution, sat down.

"Unfortunately, Gloria was called away on short notice," Faith told the audience. "That means fewer chances for you to interact with her, and we regret that. So does she. But the good news is that we expect her back before the end of the week. And the better news is that now we have more opportunity to get to know Jed and Tanya. This is an informal hour of chat, no moderator. They'll start with a discussion of suspense, and I'm sure we'll be on the edges of our seats, wondering where they'll go from there. Ladies and gentlemen, without further ado, Tanya Race and Jed Knowlan."

Tanya and Jed thanked Faith at the same time, one on top of the other. Faith couldn't understand anything either of them said beyond their names.

"Do I need to stay and act as referee?" Faith asked, earning a laugh from the audience.

Jed sat back with his hands up, a broad grin on his face. "I surrender," he said.

Tanya's somewhat forced smile warmed up. She sat forward and turned an even warmer smile on the audience.

"But if I can jump in for thirty seconds here," Jed said, plowing over whatever Tanya had been about to say. "Believe me when I say that I'm a complete fan of strong women characters in thrillers and suspense novels."

"Wonderful," Tanya said, giving him a withering glare.

"Just as I'm a fan of the women who write them."

"That's—"

Jed didn't let Tanya finish that sentence either. "What I'm trying to say is that I'm happy to follow your lead in this chat."

"Are you?" Tanya asked coldly.

"I am. Take it away, Tanya. Oh, but one more thing. What are we chatting about?"

"Nothing so far, unless you want to discuss the homicidal tendencies of strong women." The audience chuckled.

He put his hands up again. "This time I really do surrender."

"In that case, I think we'll get along just fine without a referee," Tanya said to more laughter from the audience.

Oh brother. Faith gladly left the stage. As she went down the steps she saw that not everyone in the audience was being entertained by the banter onstage. Charlotte was staring at the authors with . . . what? Distaste? Distrust? But was that sentiment for both of them, or was it directed at just one? Then a movement at the back of the audience caught Faith's eye. Lindsey also watched the stage, but when she saw Faith watching her, she slipped out of the room.

Faith puzzled over Lindsey's presence until she saw her friend Brooke, the sous-chef, come in through the door Lindsey had just gone out. Brooke straightened the cloths on a couple of tables at the back of the audience. *Of course—the refreshment tables.* There would be a break partway through the chat unless the audience was so thoroughly in suspense over what the authors would say or do next that they wouldn't leave their seats. Why was Faith suspicious of Lindsey? The woman had probably just put the cloths on the tables.

Brooke waved to Faith. Now would be a good time for a quick word with Brooke and Midge, Faith realized. Midge was still sitting at the end of a row and Faith hurried down that side of the audience. "I've got news and a favor to ask," she whispered to Midge. "Follow me." Without hesitating or asking questions, Midge followed her to the back of the room where Brooke was.

"I'm going to sound like one of Tanya's or Jed's characters," Faith said to her friends. Brooke and Midge looked at each other and then leaned in close.

"Do tell," Brooke said.

"Bare bones only for now, but can you make it to the Candle House for a special meeting of the book club? I'll fill you in there."

"You've been studying up on the elements of suspense, I see," Midge said with a quiet laugh.

"It sounds that way, doesn't it? Let's hope this turns out to be as much fiction as our authors put on paper. In the meantime, I'd like you to keep your ears open for talk around the manor about Gloria."

"Eavesdropping on guests?" Brooke asked, a little more loudly than Faith would have liked. She immediately put a hand over her mouth, then moved it long enough to mouth "Sorry," and put it back.

Faith peeked over her shoulder. The audience seemed to be captivated by whatever Tanya was telling them. "Guests or staff," Faith said. "Or anybody. Put that way, it doesn't sound very nice, does it?"

"You mean apart from it sounding like there's more to Gloria's absence than you're letting on?" Midge studied Faith's face. "There is, but you can't tell us, right?"

"If there is, then she can't tell us that either," Brooke said with perfect logic. "Is there anything in particular we're listening for?"

Faith shook her head. "Anything and everything for now. And I don't mean you should skulk around corners or anything. If it makes you uncomfortable—"

Brooke waved the idea of discomfort aside and Midge shook her head.

"I need to get the refreshments organized and out here for the break," Brooke said, "so I'll get started right now."

"And I'll get started later," Midge said. "I've got a rare morning off and I want to hear these two one-upping each other some more. I'll see you at the break." She gave Faith's shoulder a squeeze and went back to her seat.

Tanya and Jed had relaxed into a real conversation, almost as if they'd forgotten they were onstage. Faith heard very little shifting of feet or rattling of programs. The authors' words seemed to have woven a spell on the audience. Faith moved to the side of the room so she could see faces and not just the backs of heads.

Charlotte was still there, nearer the stage. Faith wished that she dared to move so she could see Charlotte's face again. Was she still staring daggers at the authors, or was she enjoying herself? Had Aunt Eileen phoned her yet?

Alyssa was still in the audience too and sitting as still as the rest. Did she suspect something, or had Faith successfully tamped down the woman's concerns? Or did Alyssa *know* something? Faith decided she'd better take Alyssa aside during the break and see if she could find out what, if anything, she did know about Gloria's absence, without alerting her to the true nature of the situation. Not that Faith even knew what the true situation was.

Faith found herself as caught up in the wide-ranging conversation between Tanya and Jed as the rest of the audience. She was also as surprised as anyone, Tanya and Jed included, when Marlene appeared onstage and interrupted them to announce the refreshment break. Alyssa was one of the first in the audience on her feet. Faith moved to intercept her.

But first she had to stand aside and let the audience stream past. After last night's reception and breakfast this morning, the guests didn't need a second invitation to anything coming from the Castleton Manor kitchen. A woman leaving the row nearest Faith approached her. She stretched one arm and then the other over her head and shook out her legs, giving Faith the idea that her yoga pants, tank top, and running shoes were for more than show.

"How were these particular authors chosen for this week of programs?" the woman asked. "Excuse me a minute. I don't often sit still for that long." She turned, put her fingertips on the wall, and did half a dozen standing push-ups. "I have a rule. For every ten minutes I sit I do at least a minute of stretching and loosening up. It helps me refocus my energy." She shook her arms out, then abruptly bent over, grabbed her ankles, pressed her forehead to her knees, and came upright again. She blew limp bangs out of her eyes, crossed her arms, and turned to face Faith. "What I'm getting at with my question about the authors is this: What if the group you bring in doesn't get along? At all? Do you vet them in advance? Do you ask for references? Who makes the choices and who makes the decisions? You?"

"No. The work on Simmering Suspense Week began a year or more ago," Faith said. "I've only been here a few months."

"Huh. Too bad." The woman rolled her right shoulder three times, then her left, and walked away.

Faith couldn't tell if the woman was happy or unhappy about the authors or her answers. Or maybe she was just curious and looking for information. Faith turned to look for Alyssa and almost bumped into Marlene.

"Did you remind that guest that we have a gym at her disposal?" Marlene asked. She leaned close to the wall where the woman had done her push-ups. "She might have left fingerprints."

"Any news from Gloria?" Faith asked.

"No. And quite frankly, I'm disappointed. I expected better from her. She has a reputation for being very professional."

"So, what do you do when you have a signed contract and the author doesn't follow through?"

"I discussed the options with Charlotte," Marlene said. "She is *deeply* disappointed, but she doesn't want to make a fuss. And she's right. We need to know when to choose our battles, and we don't want bad publicity. Not that we couldn't handle it."

"You do a great job with the press," Faith said.

"You think so?" Marlene looked honestly surprised, and Faith was glad she could give an honest answer.

"No question."

"Really? Thank you, Faith."

Faith tried not to show her own surprise. Marlene didn't often thank her. Thanks seemed to get caught in her prickles, but maybe Faith's compliment had smoothed those prickles for the time being. And then she realized it worked both ways. Complimenting and thanking were both simple kindnesses. If she made an effort to offer either to Marlene more often, then maybe their relationship would improve.

Marlene joined the crowd heading for the refreshment table. Faith didn't see Alyssa in that direction. She didn't see her at the table, either. Then she heard Alyssa's now-familiar voice and saw her talking to Tanya and Jed. The three of them were grouped near the French doors leading to the terrace, Tanya and Jed facing each other and Alyssa almost between them. Faith wondered why they hadn't moved away from Alyssa, then realized that with the unhappy expression on Alyssa's face and her hands on her hips, she'd created an effective barrier. Faith reluctantly turned her back on the refreshments and went to see if she could be of any help to the authors.

"Of course I'm aggravated," Alyssa was saying when Faith reached the group. Alyssa acknowledged Faith by turning to her and adding, "And I don't think I'll be asking for too much if I want some sort of compensation."

"For Gloria's absence," Tanya said to Faith. "She's upset."

"And immensely disappointed," Alyssa said.

Faith could picture how upset and *monumentally* disappointed Marlene would be if Alyssa voiced her idea and it took hold among the rest of the guests. "We do hope Gloria will be back before the end of the week," she said.

"I'm not sure it matters at this point," Alyssa said. "I'm seriously thinking of leaving. Not that I have anything against you two, but I haven't read any of your books and this week isn't turning out to be the way it was advertised. Do you think they'll give me a refund for the rest of the week?" she asked Faith. "If they can't explain Gloria's absence, they have to, don't they?"

"I can find out for you," Faith said, "but that's really a question for Marlene Russell."

"You sent me to Marlene this morning when I first told you Gloria was missing. She gave me no information whatsoever."

"She probably had no information to give, and I'm sorry about that. But she is the one you'll need to talk to." Faith looked for Marlene at the refreshment table and didn't see her. "You might have to catch her in her office later. Oh, there she is. Near that potted palm."

Alyssa looked toward the palm. "Thank you. Well. Yes. That's good to know. Maybe I'll let her enjoy her refreshments first." She leaned closer to Faith. "Marlene wasn't exactly warm and fuzzy when I talked to her this morning." She looked at Marlene again and then headed for the refreshment table at the opposite end of the room.

"There goes the kind of fan who gives fanaticism a bad name," Jed said.

"Gloria's partly to blame for that," said Tanya. "She gives struggling authors a bad name."

"That is not true," Jed said.

"Yeah," Tanya said. "Right."

"I *am* right."

Their back-and-forth sounded like an argument they'd had before, not to mention somewhat childish. Faith wondered how well they actually knew each other. She was about to leave them for the refreshment table when one of the French doors swung open and two blurs of fur streaked into the room. The first, black and white and tailless, was immediately followed by the second—red-brown and yapping.

"Watson?" Faith said. "Watson!"

The two zipped around the perimeter of the room, the dog gaining on Watson. Watson skidded into a curve, then, regaining his feet, changed tactics. He poured everything he had into a dash for the refreshment table. He reached it and dove for safety under the table skirt. The dog, still barking and perhaps confused by Watson's disappearance, made a flying leap. With a final yip, it landed in the middle of the table, all four paws in a fresh apple strudel.

6

In the shocked silence after the dog vaulted onto the refreshment table and stuck its landing in the strudel as well as any Olympic athlete, everyone heard the man responsible for it.

"Look what followed me home," he said with a forced laugh. He looked ready to back out the still-open door. "What do you think? Can I keep them?"

"Now that it's too late," Marlene said coldly, "please close the door."

"Oh. Right. The dog just followed me up from the beach. Sorry about that. And sorry about that too." He pointed to the ruined refreshments.

The dog had set about sampling as many of the other treats as it could reach, running from one end of the table to the other. How it managed to dodge the hands of so many trying to catch it, Faith didn't know. The dog also ignored every command to sit, stay, or stop.

"Why can't they catch him?" Marlene demanded. "How can Midge call herself a veterinarian and not be able to control that little vandal?" Rather than help, Marlene backed farther away from the scene of destruction.

Faith had never seen Marlene at such a loss. She seemed to have lost her starch, to be sagging. Faith grabbed a chair and guided Marlene into it. Then, when the dog-catching action moved to the other end of the table, she stooped to look under the table skirt. Watson greeted her with a lazy blink. He'd folded himself into a neat loaf shape toward the middle of the space under the table where feet wouldn't reach him. He appeared unhurt. He also showed no concern for the hubbub going on over and around him.

"Were you being tormented, or were you having a morning lark?" Faith asked. "And is that dog who I think it is?"

Watson yawned.

From above, Faith heard a triumphant "Got him!" She told Watson to behave himself and stood back up. Brooke, whose culinary creations were in a shambles, held the dog in her arms.

"After all that rabble-rousing, you're just going to collapse in my arms?" Brooke looked at the dog. It was hardly bigger than an armful. It licked her hand and closed its eyes. "I don't know whether to cry or laugh," she said.

"Or put him back outside?" The man who'd let the animals in hadn't moved from the French door.

"Please put him back outside," Marlene said.

"Someone must be looking for him by now." The man put his hand on the knob. "I feel terrible about all this. If Mrs. Jaxon were here, she'd skin me alive. Has anyone seen the poor cat?"

"What cat?" Marlene asked.

"The cat got away," Faith said. She scanned the room for Charlotte rather than meet Marlene's eyes. Charlotte must have left before the rumpus.

"We probably shouldn't put this guy out," said Brooke. She cradled the dog in the crook of one arm and held its tag so she could read it. "'It' is 'he,' and his name is Sir Arfer Conan Doyle. He belongs to Gloria Bauer."

"I knew it!" Alyssa shouted. "This is proof that something's happened to Gloria." She pointed at Faith, then swiveled until she located Marlene, still sitting in the chair, and jabbed a finger at her too. "This dog is evidence. Gloria would not let him run loose."

Jed shook his head. "Gloria's dog is a known escape artist. She told me she chased him halfway to Fort Myers from Orlando last month."

"So where is she?" Alyssa asked. "Why isn't she chasing him now? Did *you* see her?" she asked the man Sir Arfer had followed. "Did you hear her calling him?"

"Afraid not."

"He's a terrier," Jed said. "A young one." Jed might have taken lessons from Watson in how to look unconcerned. "Young terriers run faster than most women Gloria's age. Especially if she's wearing the wrong shoes to run. If the dog is proof of anything, he's proof Gloria's fine. She was probably out walking him."

"It's a conspiracy to keep the truth from us."

"Conspiracies are like happy endings," Jed said. "They only happen in books."

Faith glanced sharply at Jed. What had he meant by that?

"And truth is often stranger than fiction," Alyssa snapped back. "Someone should go down to the beach to look for Gloria."

"Are you offering?" Jed asked.

Alyssa huffed and walked away.

"I told you," a woman near Faith said to a group of other women she was standing with. "That woman is an actress. She's part of the program."

"The bit with the dog was over the top," another woman said. "I wanted some of that strudel."

"I'm sure they'll bring more out," the first woman said.

"Not as long as the chef is holding the dog."

Tanya had stayed out of the dog-catching fray, but she went over to Brooke and Sir Arfer now. "What a sweet baby," she said. "Why don't I take him for you?"

"Our vet went to get a leash," Brooke said. "I kind of hate

to take the chance he'll get loose again." Sir Arfer lay like a limp noodle in her arms. But he was a strudel-covered noodle and there was still plenty of damage he could do, on the table or loose in the manor.

"Well, if you're sure, but who's just a big cutie?"

Sir Arfer, who might have been dozing, opened his eyes when Tanya leaned close and cooed to him. He yipped and Tanya jumped back.

"Sorry, sweetie," Tanya said. "Did I startle you?" She held her hand out to him.

Sir Arfer started barking in earnest. He didn't struggle to get out of Brooke's arms, but she carried him away from the table—and Tanya. Faith joined her and they moved farther from the crowd.

"You're just in time," Brooke said when Midge arrived with the leash. "This little rascal's had too much partying for one day."

Midge and the dog treat she'd brought with her made friends with Sir Arfer. She clipped the lead to his collar and took him from Brooke.

"Folks," Brooke said, "you've all been good sports. We'll get the mess cleaned up and have more refreshments brought out as quickly as we can."

"Do you offer doggy bags?" one of the guests called.

Even Marlene cracked a smile at that. Faith decided it wasn't the best time to tell Marlene about Alyssa's request for compensation. Let Alyssa do that if she was serious about it. And she obviously wasn't that serious, because she was in her seat in the front row, waiting for the program to continue. Now, while Alyssa was alone, might be a good time to find out if she did know anything about Gloria. *But that might just rile her up again.*

Faith glanced over and saw that the man who'd let the animals in looked more relaxed. He leaned a shoulder against the frame of the French door, hands in his trouser pockets, talking to Jed. The tweed suit he wore made him look slightly out of place, as though he belonged on another continent or in another time. He was probably in his midthirties, a decade or so younger than Jed, but they appeared to be enjoying each other's company. Judging by Jed's arm movements, he was telling a whopper of a fish story. But before he could reel in his catch, they were interrupted by Charlotte Jaxon.

Charlotte greeted both men, Jed with a smile, the younger man with surprise that turned into a quick hug. To Faith, it looked like the greeting of old friends. Charlotte said something. She listened to one and then the other, stepping back when Jed added gestures directing her attention to the cleaning operation.

Then Charlotte froze.

Is she staring at the mess? Faith wondered. *At the staff?* Brooke and three others were clearing away the debris. Among the three was Lindsey.

Jed seemed to be trying to get Charlotte's attention. Charlotte glanced at him, then away. The young man, his hands back in his pockets, said something. Charlotte turned away and came toward Faith, who braced herself for whatever reaction Charlotte might have. But Charlotte passed right by her, leaving the Great Hall and going into the gallery. Faith stepped to another of the archways between the two rooms and saw Charlotte going toward the library.

What if she wants to retrieve the ransom note? Faith wondered. *What will she think when she doesn't find it?*

7

Faith wanted to follow Charlotte, but first she sought out Marlene. Depending on what happened in the library with Charlotte, she couldn't be sure she'd be back in time to introduce the second half of the author chat. She saw Marlene talking with a couple of guests at the base of the grand staircase and rushed over.

"Marlene? Hi, sorry to interrupt." Faith wasn't sorry. She'd learned that approaching Marlene with potentially unpleasant news tended to be safer in a group situation, even if that meant barging into the middle of a conversation. Marlene behaved better in front of witnesses. "I wanted to let you know that I need to check on something in the library. I'll try to be back in a few minutes, but if I'm not, can you round up Tanya and Jed—"

"Oh sure, I'll be fine," Marlene said with a wave.

Faith, already on her way to the gallery, called thanks over her shoulder. Of course by the time she reached the gallery, Charlotte was out of sight. Faith started for the library anyway. Unless Charlotte had gone outside, that was the logical place to look for her. But someone called her name. She looked over her shoulder, and she couldn't pretend she didn't see the woman waving at her to stop.

"I was afraid I'd miss you," the woman said.

"The tour? You haven't missed it." Faith did her best to sound polite but in a hurry. "It isn't until two."

"Not interested," the woman said. "Oh! I didn't mean it like that. I love libraries. But it's you I didn't want to miss. We spoke earlier. Rachel Vail."

The woman stuck her hand out and Faith shook it. She didn't recognize Rachel Vail, but her voice—*wait*. Yes, she did recognize her. This was the woman who'd been wearing yoga pants and doing stretches after the first half of the chat.

"Nice to see you again," Faith said.

Rachel seemed happier to see Faith than she had been earlier, although maybe she'd been preoccupied with stretching at that point. Now she looked as though she might be on her way to an interview or a professional appointment. She'd changed out of her yoga clothes into black stovepipe trousers and a deep purple jacket with a mandarin collar.

"I'm on my way—" Faith took a step and pointed an index finger down the gallery toward the library.

"And I don't want to keep you. I'll walk with you."

Faith stopped. If she found Charlotte in the library and it wasn't already too late, she wanted to speak to her alone. "That's all right. What can I do for you?"

Rachel put herself in front of Faith, looking just as happy to stop and stand as to tag along. "As I'm sure you know," she said, "I'm the author of the Emmy Lilly suspense novels."

Faith didn't know, but she didn't want to disappoint Rachel's hopeful smile. "Oh, of course. You're *that* Rachel Vail." She made a mental note to look her up later.

"You've read my books?" Rachel asked.

"Not yet, but they're on my to-read pile."

"I can't tell you how much that tickles me." Rachel's smile was broad enough that her molars were visible, and Faith promised herself she really would look up the books.

"Now, I know you need to get going," Rachel said, "but I wanted you to see that I clean up reasonably well."

"Sorry?"

Rachel held her arms out like model. "I go from fitness to finery in fewer than fifteen minutes."

"And you look great." *Where was this going?* Faith looked down the hall toward the library. She didn't see Charlotte leaving it. *Good.*

"Thanks," Rachel said. "After talking to you at the break, I ran up and down one of the back stairways a few times to get my respiration going. Then I went to my room and had a power shower and changed."

"So you missed the, uh, the kerfuffle?" She was going to miss Charlotte, she just knew it.

"Not interested. I don't do sweets."

"Oh, but kerfuffle isn't—"

"That's okay," Rachel said. "No between-meal snacks either."

"Is there something I can do for you, Rachel? I really do need to—" Faith snuck another step down the hall.

"It's something I can do for you. A way to make up for Gloria's absence. A way to help us both out. Shall I cut to the chase?"

"If you can do it at a sprint."

"Track and field star at Emerson," Rachel said, throwing her shoulders back. "That's not what you meant, and that doesn't help in this situation, but because I'm another suspense writer in residence, I'm probably the only one who *can* help you out, because I'm willing to take Gloria's place for the rest of the week."

Did I actually not see that coming? Faith asked herself. *Because I really should have seen that coming.* "That's certainly an idea, Rachel, and generous of you. I'm not the one who would make that decision, though."

"But you can tell me who would make the decision. And you can tell me if that's the same person to whom I should speak concerning payment for filling in on such short notice."

"We're hoping Gloria will be back, you know. Soon." *And the sooner the better.*

"But in the meantime, as a friend and a fan, maybe you can put in a good word for me."

After making no promises but giving Marlene's name to Rachel, Faith barely kept herself from running to the library. *To show her what a sprint looks like,* she grumbled to herself. *I shouldn't have stopped when she called my name. It is possible to be polite without being a pushover. I should take lessons in standing firm and going my own way from Watson. And just for that, Rachel Vail's books are not going on my to-read pile.*

Wolfe Jaxon was standing with a foot on one of the rolling ladders and his nose in a book when Faith steamed into the library. He marked his place in the book. "Good morning. This is a pleasant surprise. I thought you'd be tied up with the program."

"I was. I still should be." *And I knew it. Charlotte isn't here.*

"How's it going? It's the chat this morning, isn't it? Is Jed keeping everyone entertained?"

"Jed?" Faith looked around for Charlotte anyway, walking to where she could see each of the wingback chairs, just in case. "Sure. He's doing his part, but Tanya's holding her own. Was your mother here just now?"

"She was, but she didn't seem particularly happy to see me either. Is everything all right?"

"Did she say anything?" *Great. Could I be any ruder?* "Do you know where she went?" *Apparently I can.* "I'm sorry, Wolfe—"

His phone rang. He pulled it from his pocket and checked the display.

"Just a minute, Faith. I have to take this. Hey, Blake," he said, greeting his brother. "Hold on a second, will you?" He muffled the phone against his chest and spoke to Faith. "Sorry, I have to go." He put the phone back to his ear and turned away, crossing to the farthest side of the library and out of her earshot.

Great. But maybe, just maybe, Charlotte circled around on the terrace and went back to the Main Hall.

Faith waited for a few seconds to see if Wolfe would turn around again. If he did, she'd wave. He didn't, but she caught a movement out of the corner of her eye. It was Watson tiptoeing into the room. She watched as he sniffed the air, then crossed to the chair nearest to Wolfe. She waved to him instead and left him cleaning his ears with a fastidious paw.

The cat felt entitled to a nap after the strenuous game of chase he and the dog had played. A snack would be nice too. The canine had shown unexpected intelligence when he leaped onto the table and helped himself. The cat had heard him running from one end of the table to the other. Making a spectacle of himself. Exhibiting no finesse. And yapping. The never-ending yapping. It was always the same with dogs. The cat would have considered the perpetual inferiority of dogs a pity, but their state didn't interest him. A long, luxurious nap—that interested him. The velvet armchairs in the library had almost certainly been made with cats in mind. If only the man with the phone didn't sound so angry.

After the man with the angry phone call had left, the cat was only able to doze and dream for a few hours. Then a group of the people who traipsed around the manor—and who were well and frequently fed—came into the library. Some of them smelled faintly of seafood. That interested him, but their talking and twittering laughter did not.

8

"Shh," Faith said. "We're in a library."

People were still trickling in for the afternoon tour, but those who'd gathered around her laughed and hushed one another. She liked to start tours in front of the fireplace. Many of their guests were current or former librarians and booksellers, and a stay at Castleton Manor was a dream vacation for them. She'd even heard a few say that the manor was on their bucket list of beautiful libraries to visit. And the fireplace was mentioned as a feature that helped elevate the library to bucket list status.

For the tour that afternoon she had about a dozen guests, including Jed and Tanya. And Alyssa. Seeing her gave Faith a moment of unease, but Alyssa appeared calm and greeted her pleasantly. She also seemed to have become quite chummy with Tanya. Rachel Vail wasn't there. Maybe she'd been successful and had talked Marlene into letting her substitute for Gloria. If she had, Faith wondered how that would change the tetchy dynamics between Jed and Tanya. *And how will Alyssa react to Gloria being replaced?*

"I wonder if that's the daredevil cat from the great race." A man at the edge of the group was looking at Watson, who was sitting up in one of the chairs near the fireplace. Watson yawned, waking from his nap. When the man turned toward Faith, she realized he was the one who'd let Watson and Sir Arfer in through the French door. "He's missing most of his tail," the man said. "That couldn't have happened this morning, could it?"

"He lost it when he was a kitten," Faith said.

"Because I'd never forgive myself."

"I'm sure Watson is happy to hear you say so, but he doesn't really like having attention drawn to his . . . situation."

"Completely understandable," the man said.

The cat looked down his nose at the people staring at him. There were too many of them and too many more important things to be doing. He leaped from the chair, knowing he looked both sleek and dignified—and nothing at all like that yappy dog had with his ostentatious jumping and prancing—then turned his back on the rude gapers and left the room.

"Forget roasting an ox in the fireplace," a woman said when Faith offered that comparison. "It's big enough to be a whole new wing on our public library back home."

"Where's home?" Faith asked.

"Blue Plum, Tennessee. And I'm exaggerating. The fireplace would only be big enough to be a quiet reading room. A warm one."

"And snug," Faith said. "It's nice to have you here."

"But has anyone done a fact check on that claim?" Jed asked. "Because you hear that about big fireplaces, but has anyone ever really roasted an ox in one?"

"Not in this one, I hope," the woman from Tennessee said. "The smoke and—what would it be? The fat, the tallow—whatever it should be called—the *grease* would be terrible for the collection."

"Well obviously, I didn't mean this one," Jed said. "But I'm serious. Do you know how big an ox is?"

"I know how big a windbag is," Tanya said under her breath. Jed didn't give any indication that he heard her, but Alyssa snickered beside Tanya.

"Let's move over to the special collections, shall we?" Faith put herself between Jed and Tanya, just in case, and led the group to the locked glass cabinets housing the most valuable books in the library. "When Captain Angus Jaxon built Castleton Manor, he literally and figuratively laid the foundations for the fine collection of books we have today. He had a love for good literature and fine craftsmanship, and he had an uncanny sense for when an unsung author or illustrator was worth supporting. That's why we're lucky enough to have one of the most amazing editions of illustrated *Grimm's Fairy Tales* ever published."

Faith slipped a set of small keys from her pocket, ignoring the ransom note she'd tucked there. The lavender paper still felt heavy in her pocket, but she wasn't going to let that imaginary weight bring down the pleasure of showing off the books in this case. As she fitted one of the keys into the lock of the middle cabinet, she didn't try to hide her grin.

"Treasure," Tanya said. "You're opening a treasure chest."

"Exactly," Faith said. "And it feels that way every single time. Prepare to be in awe. Or maybe you'll experience that rare phenomenon called love at first sight." She dropped the keys back into her pocket and then slid open a shallow drawer beneath the cabinet. From it she took a pair of white cotton gloves. She pulled them on, opened the cabinet door, and removed a leather-bound book the size of a modern paperback mystery but as thick as three or four of them put together. She showed them the tooled artwork on the cover—delicate lines depicting a pathway winding into a forest. Then she held the book flat on the palms of her hands. *Like an offering*, she thought, adding aloud, "Look, but please don't touch."

She smiled when she heard several reverent gasps.

"This is the work of Michael Patrick," Faith continued. "He was a Cape Cod artist, born within eyesight of the lighthouse in Truro, down toward the end of the Cape, in 1867. He lived there, in the house where he was born, until he passed away in 1954. He worked as an illustrator for a number of magazines in the first half of the twentieth century. He made a reasonable living at it, but he wasn't as well known as one of his contemporaries whose name you probably recognize, Norman Rockwell. I agree with Captain Jaxon—Michael Patrick's work deserves recognition. And in a purely personal aside, I prefer it to Rockwell's."

"It isn't as sentimental as Rockwell's," Tanya observed.

"You're right. Patrick did more landscapes and outdoor scenes than families and small-town life. Although he also did those, and he seemed to have a soft spot for illustrations of women knitting. He managed to include a cat in most of them. So you know his work, Tanya?"

"I saw a retrospective at a gallery in Provincetown a few years ago," Tanya said. "I don't remember seeing books in the exhibit, though, or reading about book illustrations."

"The cool thing is that he didn't just illustrate books. He made them as well." Faith turned the book over so they could see that Patrick had tooled another view of the forest and winding path on the back and a gnarled tree trunk on the spine. Then she opened the book to show the endpapers—watercolors done from inside the forest and looking along a path toward a sunlit meadow. "Illustrating for magazines paid the bills," Faith said, "but handmade books were his passion." She turned to the title page. "There are six books in Patrick's folk- and fairy-tale series. Each book is one of a kind and full of absolutely brilliant watercolors. He made three sets of two each."

"And Castleton Manor is lucky enough to own one book?" Alyssa asked.

Faith shook her head and held up two fingers. "We are very lucky indeed."

"Do you grant visiting privileges for the *Grimm's*?" Tanya asked. "I'd love to look at it more closely."

"Sure, that can be arranged. Anyone interested is welcome to set up a time with me." Faith put the book back in the cabinet, locked the door, and stripped off the cotton gloves. "We have other treasures too. The entire collection is cataloged, so you can browse the shelves, browse the computer, or even browse an honest-to-goodness card catalog."

"What are they worth?" Jed asked. "A set of Patrick's books?"

"Believe it or not, I don't know. Librarians, archivists, and museum curators aren't encouraged to think in terms of dollar amounts."

"Ballpark figure? Come on, best guess."

"They're kept under lock and key," Alyssa said. "Doesn't that tell you enough?"

"You got a problem with curiosity?" Jed asked.

"Speaking of curiosity," Faith said, stepping between Jed and Alyssa, "did you know the library has a wonderful collection of fables and folktales about cats? Let me show you." She took Jed's arm and led the group to the other side of the library, walking slowly and telling them about other collections, the woodwork, and the frescoed ceiling as they walked.

The man who'd let Watson and Sir Arfer into the Great Hall stayed behind in the library after the tour.

"Have you been reading Captain Jaxon's magic and misdirection collection?" he asked. "Because that was a neat bit of misdirection you used on Jed." He put his hand out. "Heath Westcott," he said as Faith shook it.

"I'm glad to finally know your name. Otherwise I would have had to keep thinking of you as 'the man who let chaos into the author chat.'"

"That was fairly awful, wasn't it?"

"Did the dog really follow you home?"

"From the beach. No idea where he came from. Or the cat. I actually thought the dog had turned around and headed back toward the beach, and I didn't think anything more about it. When I opened the door I had no idea he'd seen the cat and changed course. Have he and Gloria been reunited yet?"

"I haven't heard."

"But someone will have contacted her so she'll know where he is?"

"I'm sure Midge—Midge Foster, the vet—is taking good care of him, and she'll do what she can to get them back together."

"Good. No real harm done, then, I hope," Heath said. "Nice tour, by the way."

"Thanks."

"You got everything almost right."

"What did I get wrong?"

"Oh, don't worry about it. There's almost no way you could know anything about what I'm referring to."

"You make it sound very mysterious."

"I'm part of a small and select circle. You think I'm pompous, don't you?"

"I didn't," Faith said with a laugh. "But are you?"

"I certainly like to think so. But I'm also willing to let you in on the secret of the *true* facts, so maybe I'm not so bad after all. Would you like to hear the story?"

"Very much."

"The claim that the fireplace is big enough to roast an ox is accurate, and it was proven. Or it was proven as accurately as it could be, using a test devised by a couple of twelve-year-old boys and a St. Bernard. An unharmed St. Bernard, I hasten to add. We returned the dog in exactly the same condition as we found it when we borrowed it."

"Borrowed? Or is that 'borrowed'?" Faith asked, making air quotes.

"With the air quotes, definitely. And not to sound like the victim in all this, but we sacrificed a lot for science that day. In terms of St. Bernard drool, anyway. Trust me. You don't want to hear about the drool."

"'We'?"

"Blake Jaxon, black sheep of the otherwise esteemed Jaxon family, and I. I'd tell you that I'm a family friend, but I only spent a few idyllic summers here. And not everyone in the family feels all that friendly toward me."

"Because of the St. Bernard?"

"And I'm sure now because of Gloria Bauer's terrorist terrier. I seem to have a failing where dogs are concerned."

"But you're here as a guest this week," Faith said. "That doesn't sound like anyone holds a grudge against you."

"It's possible I've exaggerated. Charlotte raised three boys, which I think necessitates a forgiving soul. It helps that I've become respectable."

"And what makes you respectable?"

"I'm a bookseller. I have a card somewhere here to prove it." He patted up and down his jacket with both hands, frowning in apparent concern. Then he snapped his fingers near Faith's head and produced his card as if he'd found it behind her ear. "Blake and I read most of the magic books here one of those summers." He handed the card to her. "But what could be more respectable than a bookseller? Well, other than a librarian."

"Certainly not a magician," Faith said with a smile. "But I'll overlook the magician part because some of my favorite places are libraries and bookstores."

"It makes me happy to hear you say that. See you around."

Faith strapped on her backpack and rode her bicycle to the library in town that afternoon. Watson sat in the basket between the handlebars. The rain had moved through, but November would bring colder weather soon.

"Let's take advantage of every bit of sun while we can, Watson," she said as they wheeled along the wooded lane toward town. "We can't stay too long, though. It's getting dark earlier and earlier, plus I have more work to do to fix the holes Gloria left in our program schedule."

Watson leaned forward in the basket.

"Faster?" Faith asked. "I'll pedal as fast as I can, Mr. Speed Demon." She hadn't expected the move to Lighthouse Bay to have such a good effect on the old cat. Not that he was old, but at fourteen he was no spring kitten. They'd lived in an apartment in Boston before moving to the Cape, and over those years he'd settled into the quiet life of an aging pet in the big city. And whatever number life he was on now, he seemed to be having the absolute time of it.

"I'm glad Sir Arfer turned up this morning, even if he did chase you. It gives me hope that we'll get Gloria back too."

Watson's ears twitched.

"Was that a comment or a bug in your ear?" Faith asked. Then she heard the car, its tires squealing as it navigated the curves behind them too fast.

They'd been riding on the narrow, paved shoulder, but Faith steered the bike off the asphalt altogether and bumped along in the scrubby grass between the road and the woods. She wondered briefly about poison ivy and then chanced a look over her shoulder. A hundred yards behind, the car squealed into view, skidding as it came around the bend. The driver fought the skid, seemed to regain control, and then left the pavement and came straight at them.

9

"Hang on, Watson!"

Faith wrenched the bike's handlebars to the right and pedaled for the woods. Fractured thoughts flashed through her head: *sharp angle—out of the path—into the trees—tree!*

The bicycle missed the tree by a cat's whisker and ended up in a tangle of vines. Watson jumped clear of the basket and ran into the woods. Faith untangled herself, called him, and ran back to the road, but the car hadn't stopped and was long gone. *The car.* Could she remember anything about it? Only that it was being driven by an idiot. *Small? Gray? Like a million other cars on the road.* She didn't even know if the driver was male or female, or if there had been more than one person in the car. In other words, she had nothing.

Faith called Watson again. She checked to see if she'd scraped herself or impaled herself on thorns. Just scratches, but they didn't matter. Faith pulled the bike out of the vegetation and began pulling vines from the spokes. She called Watson again. He knew his way around and had gotten himself into town on his own before, so she wasn't worried. What did worry her was the awful idea that maybe her "accident" wasn't really an accident.

The Candle House Library, although privately funded, was the public library in Lighthouse Bay. The Jaxon family had given the three-story stone building to the town several decades earlier. It was originally the site for a small-scale candle manufacturing business, hence its name. The building had been renovated on the inside, but it retained many characteristics of the old candle house, as well as its charm.

"You're sure you're all right?" Eileen asked after Faith told her about the incident. They were in Eileen's office. "Sit down."

Faith shook her head. "No, I'm fine. My heart's fine and now I know my adrenaline level is more than adequate. Of course, it's possible my imagination works overtime. I'm sure the car wasn't really trying to hit me."

"Did you really think it was? I can see how you might, but . . . are you sure you're all right?"

"You already asked me that. And yes, I am. And yes, I did think it was, if I was thinking anything at all. But it was one of those situations that starts out in slow motion and then shifts into warp speed, and you only catch the tail end of whatever thoughts go zipping through your mind. So no, of course someone wasn't trying to hit me."

"Not just someone," Eileen said. "Someone from the manor or who'd been there. That road doesn't go anywhere else."

"Sure it does. It goes on down through the woods."

"Have you ever gone that way?"

"Watson and I walked a little way down it. But we were still new here, and Watson wasn't too sure about taking long country walks yet."

"You didn't go far enough, then. The road is private beyond the manor and it dead-ends a mile or so into the woods."

"A paved dead-end road? Well, if it belongs to the Jaxons, I guess that doesn't really surprise me."

"They don't do things halfway, do they? The road's been there as long as I can remember. What I heard is that back before World War II, they'd planned to build another house down there in the woods. Sort of a fairy-tale cottage in a clearing. It's too bad it never happened. Wouldn't you love to see the Jaxons' idea of a fairy-tale cottage? All carved wood and thatch, mullioned windows, and roses climbing over the door? Their inspiration might have come straight out of the Cotswolds or the Black Forest."

"Or an Arthur Rackham illustration." Faith knew what her aunt was doing and thanked her.

"For what, honey?"

"For the image of a fairy-tale cottage and time to calm down."

"Not that there's any excuse for that kind of driving," Eileen said. "Just because the people who stay at a literary retreat have the good sense to love books doesn't mean they automatically have good sense for real-world living."

"I wish I'd seen the license plate. But you know, it still might have been someone who thought the road went somewhere and then got angry because it didn't. I hope Watson is okay. I looked for him for ages, but I couldn't find him anywhere." Faith did sit down then. She refused to think she'd just collapsed into the chair. And she wasn't going to cry.

Eileen picked a few leaves out of Faith's hair. "I can tell you something about that stretch where you were run off the road that I didn't know before."

"What?"

"There's Japanese honeysuckle." She showed Faith the leaves. "It grows in disturbed areas, at the edges of woods. There's been a big effort to get rid of it."

Faith appreciated this new attempt at distraction, but she was ready to get the conversation back on track. "What did you say that got Charlotte to come?"

"The truth as I know it. That you wanted her here, and that you asked me to do what I could to make it happen. That this wasn't a frivolous invitation. That you have something serious to discuss with her and the group."

"Simple, effective, and terribly foreboding. Yikes. I'm not sure *I'd* show up after an invitation like that."

"Yes you would. You're very brave," Eileen said. Her office window looked down on the street and sidewalk in front of the library. She glanced outside. "Here's Charlotte coming up the walk."

"She didn't ask what the meeting's about?"

"I didn't give her the chance. One of the first things I told her was that I didn't know what this is about either."

"Well, I'm glad it worked. Have Midge and Brooke arrived?"

"Yes. They'll meet us downstairs."

"Good. Let's go meet them and Charlotte and you'll all find out what it's about."

When Charlotte opened the door, Watson walked in ahead of her. He immediately began to twine around Faith's ankles.

"He's your cat?" Charlotte asked. "I stopped in at Happy Tails Gourmet Bakery to get something special for Gloria's dog, and I found this fellow sitting outside. I thought he might be hungry and offered him one of the biscuits I bought for Sir Arfer, but he's truly a finicky cat, isn't he? He turned his nose up at it."

"And followed you here?" Brooke asked.

"No, apparently he was coming here on his own. He walked ahead of me. He's a singular animal."

"Yes, he is." Faith could see that Watson really was fine after their scare. She picked him up anyway and cuddled him, which he didn't seem to mind. "We'll stop by Happy Tails on the way home," she told him. He rubbed his forehead against her chin.

The book club usually met after hours and sat in a semicircle of chairs pulled up to the stone fireplace, which was nearly as impressive as the one at Castleton Manor. This one was big enough for its original purpose of making candles. Today, because of the unusual circumstances, and because there was another meeting in the community room, they met in the children's program room, where they wouldn't disturb patrons with their talk. *More to the point, where we won't be overheard.*

The walls of the program room were painted so that half the room looked like a castle and the other half like a pirate ship. The artwork made Faith wish the fairy-tale cottage had come to be.

"Oh, can we have our next regular meeting in here? I want Diva and Bling to see it. They'll get a kick out of being pirates for the day," Brooke said. She frequently projected her own emotions onto her angelfish. "And Atticus would look adorable with an eye patch. Where is he?" she asked Midge.

"He seems to be having a calming effect on Sir Arfer. I left them together in one of the kennels." Atticus was Midge's Chihuahua, who usually accompanied her to meetings. When Faith first joined the club, Midge had encouraged her to bring Watson. Half the time Faith didn't need to bring Watson. He showed up on his own.

"Maybe a pirate hat," Midge said. "I don't think he'd like an eye patch. But I bet I can find a parrot for his shoulder."

Eileen brought in coffee and pumpkin spice cookies from Snickerdoodles Bakery & Tea Shop next door. "Special meeting or not, it wouldn't be our book club without something sweet. They're more spiced than sweet, though. I've already tested one."

The women sat in pint-size chairs circling a rug covered with bright Mother Goose characters. Not the kind of surroundings one would expect when discussing a kidnapping.

Charlotte thanked Midge for looking after Sir Arfer.

Midge said he was delightful but a typical young terrier. "He has more bounce per inch than a rubber ball, but I'm beginning to worry. I haven't been able to reach Gloria to return him."

"Isn't she at the manor?" Eileen asked, turning a questioning eye on her niece.

"That's why we're here," Faith said. She spoke to all of them, but she kept her eyes on Charlotte. "Gloria is missing."

"She wasn't called away?" Brooke asked. "That's what people were saying this morning."

"I don't think she was." Faith took the ransom note from her backpack. "Watson found this."

"That was addressed to me," Charlotte said. "What do you mean he found it? Where did he find it?"

"He knocked over the wastepaper basket in the library, and it must have rolled out. It was wadded into a ball. I read it."

Charlotte looked at Watson. Watson looked back at Charlotte. Faith got the impression that Charlotte wasn't entirely happy with her explanation and that she wasn't sure what to think of the cat. *Or does she distrust cats in general?* she wondered. She glanced at her cat. *If I didn't know better, I'd say Watson looks smug.*

"What's this about?" Eileen asked. "What is that letter?"

"It's about Gloria," Faith said. "Do you mind if I read it to them, Charlotte?"

They waited for Charlotte to answer. Brooke put her coffee cup down. She'd already eaten her cookie, and now she nabbed Faith's and bit into it. Stress eating was something she claimed her angelfish did when they were agitated, and she didn't seem to realize she did it herself.

When Charlotte didn't answer, Faith spoke again. "I feel like I've ambushed you with this, with the group, and I'm sorry about that. But I think we need to take this seriously." She held the note up. "And I know we can help."

"Can you?" Charlotte stared at her knees. Then she closed her eyes. When she opened them again, her shoulders relaxed. She looked at Faith and nodded.

Faith remembered every word of the note. She read aloud from the paper anyway and then looked at each of her friends in turn. "I can see by your faces that you're all as shocked as I was when I read it this morning. Brooke, you just looked over your shoulder. Because you're wondering if we *are* being watched, aren't you? We're all wondering that."

"Except me," Charlotte said. "Because it sounds exactly the way it did when I first read it." She hit the arm of her chair with her fist. "Like utter nonsense. Can you blame me for thinking it wasn't real?"

"But the amount of detail," Eileen said. "Whoever wrote it knows your name, Charlotte. They know about Gloria's necklace and our hold lockers. We use those for patrons who can't make it to the library during regular hours but want to check out a specific book. All they have to do is call us, and then we check the book out under their library card number, then put it in one of the lockers and give them a single-use access code."

"He threatened to kill her," Midge said.

"Charlotte, tell us why you didn't believe the note," Eileen said. "Why does it sound like nonsense? It sounds awfully real to me."

"Because it sounds like something out of one of her early novels, before she learned to curb her melodramatic streak. I thought she wrote the note herself and disappeared the way Agatha Christie did for two weeks."

"Christie disappeared for eleven days," Eileen said. "It was never determined exactly what happened during that time. A popular theory is that she suffered a fugue state, like temporary amnesia, brought on by her husband's affair and request for a divorce. Others claim it was a publicity stunt on her part. Do you think that's what this is?"

"I did. I was sure of it. And I was furious with her. I crumpled it into a ball and threw it out." Charlotte looked at Watson. "He really is an extraordinary cat."

Watson, sitting in Faith's lap with his paws neatly tucked, lifted his chin. Faith rubbed it and wondered why she thought Charlotte was being *too* upset. There was something odd about Charlotte's disbelief. But she really couldn't put her finger on it, and for now, Faith felt better about giving her employer the benefit of the doubt.

"What changed your mind about the letter?" Faith asked.

"The dog," Charlotte said. "Why would she leave the dog? Why hasn't she called or come looking for him?"

"May I see the letter?" Midge asked.

"Do we need to worry about fingerprints?" Brooke said.

"Charlotte's and mine are already all over it," Faith said. "How was it delivered to you, Charlotte?"

"One of the staff brought it to me. A young woman. Her fingerprints and mine will be on the envelope."

Faith passed the letter to Midge and told them the story of going to check on Gloria that morning. "I ran into Lindsey coming out of the suite. She dropped a ring of keys and a lavender envelope with Charlotte's name on it."

"That sounds right," Charlotte said. "The envelope matched the notepaper. The young woman said it arrived for me this morning."

"I assumed she found it in the suite," Faith said. She told them about finding the door unlocked and the suite empty with no signs of a struggle. "At the time I thought Gloria had packed up and left. Then Watson found the crumpled note in the library and I read it. Brooke, what do you know about Lindsey? She's new, isn't she?"

"Back up a minute," Midge said. "If anyone would know how to make something look like a kidnapping, Gloria would, right?"

"That was my belief," Charlotte said. "She's written scenes like that dozens of times."

"But the suite—the 'scene'—looks normal. How does that fit with a real kidnapping?" Midge asked. "If Gloria's been kidnapped, then how did the kidnapper get her out of her suite and a manor full of people without anyone noticing? Didn't anyone see or hear something? What about the security guard?"

"For that matter," Eileen said, "did anyone see her leave of her own free will?"

"Guests are free to come and go," Charlotte said. "And the one overnight security guard can't be everywhere at once. I actually did check to see if there were any unusual incidents reported last night. There weren't."

"It's simple," Brooke said. "It's an inside job. She's being held in one of the secret passages or hidden rooms. No one knows where they all are, do they?"

"That's an exaggeration," Charlotte said. "And fairly outlandish."

"More outlandish than Gloria's disappearance?" Faith asked. "Wolfe says he isn't sure all the secret rooms have been found."

Charlotte closed her eyes and pressed her fingertips against her forehead. "You have to understand. I don't want to believe any of this is true. I don't want it to *be* true. But yes, I have to admit it's a possibility. She could be hidden away at the manor."

"It's simple, then," Brooke said. "We'll organize a search party and go find her."

"No!" Charlotte's "no" opened her eyes, making her look as

surprised as the others at her emphatic outburst. "That would guarantee that Gloria would be put in danger. And Faith, what I don't understand is, if you believed the letter from the beginning, then why take a chance and involve this group? The letter very clearly says not to tell anyone, and *I* didn't."

"I'm so glad you didn't," Faith said. "That was my biggest worry. Okay, so I know I've taken a chance, but look at it this way. The letter tells *you* not to tell anyone—I'm just the nosy person who read your mail."

"And kidnappers' rules don't apply to snoops?" Charlotte asked.

"Not so much," Brooke said with a grin.

"Or to book clubs," Eileen said.

"What about you and your level head, Midge?" Charlotte asked. "What do you think?"

"I also think it's simple," Midge said, "but for another reason. I would trust the members of this book club with my life, and I think you should trust us to save Gloria's."

Watson hopped off Faith's lap and walked to the center of the Mother Goose rug where the Man in the Moon smiled at the ceiling. He sat in the middle of the moon, facing Charlotte and watching her.

"A singular cat," Charlotte repeated, "and a singular book club."

"You'll accept our help?" Faith asked.

"What do you propose?"

"I've been giving this a lot of thought," Faith said. She and Charlotte were across from each other in the circle. Faith put her elbows on her knees, her hands clasped, and leaned toward Charlotte. "The way I see it, we have three choices, and the kidnapper outlined two of them for us. We can comply with the note's demands and turn over the Stewart necklace. We can go to the police. Or we can ignore the kidnapper's options and try to find Gloria ourselves. And Brooke isn't so far off on sending out a search party in the manor, but that will have to be discreet. I think we can do it without looking like a posse on a search-and-recover mission."

"Ride to Gloria's rescue?" Charlotte asked. "What if she's not in the manor, or even in Lighthouse Bay? What if she's been taken off Cape Cod altogether? How will you find her? This really is my decision to make, because the letter came to me. So unless you have a very good idea where to look for her, and unless you think you can rescue her today, then I won't take any more chances. I was careless this morning when I threw the note away. As a result, not only did I put Gloria in further danger, but now you're all in danger."

"That part is my doing," Faith said, "not yours."

Charlotte shook her head. "No. It's charitable of you to let me off the hook. But I'll deliver the Stewart necklace."

"Do you know where it is?" Faith asked.

"When I spoke with security this morning, I learned that Gloria had deposited the necklace in the manor's safe when she left the reception last night. I assume that's something the kidnapper didn't bargain on and why he thinks he needs me." Charlotte rose. "Eileen, I've never used one of your hold boxes. I assume I'll need you to set the access code?"

"And to put the necklace in the box, unless you want to call me when you have. The code will only work once, so if you open the box, I'll have to reset the code for the kidnapper. For that matter, I'm not sure why the kidnapper thinks you can set the codes without someone else's help."

Charlotte looked thoughtful. "I don't know either. Maybe he—or she—thinks because the Jaxons fund the Candle House Library, I'm privy to all its secret workings." She stood. "I'll be in touch, then. But beyond that, I don't want the rest of you involved. Thank you for your offer and for your concern, but I'll handle this myself."

10

"End of meeting?" Brooke asked after Charlotte had left.

Faith nodded and flopped back in her chair. She sat forward again immediately because the back of the pint-size chair bit her spine. "Sorry about dragging all of you here and into this. Charlotte's right—it was a dangerous thing to do."

"Don't worry about it," Brooke said. "No one knows we know anything about the kidnapping."

"If it was a kidnapping. And we'll keep it quiet," said Midge. The two women got up and Midge patted Faith's knee. "Your heart's always in the right place."

"So is mine," Brooke protested. "Or it will be as soon as I run upstairs and see if I can grab a copy of the latest *Scotsman Gone* book. Now there's time travel romance the way it should be done. I'm off this evening and I plan to spend it losing my heart to the extremely splendid and kilted Tarquin Campbell."

"Let me know if it's any good," Midge called to Brooke's departing back. "You're looking blue, Faith. Is there anything I can do?"

"Get Sir Arfer to talk? Otherwise, no. I just need to spend a quiet evening with my cat, my fireplace, and my notes for tomorrow's programs. Thanks, Midge."

"I'll go set the access code on pickup box three," Eileen said. "Do you want me to call you when I hear from Charlotte?"

"Sure. Thanks. Come on, old guy. Home again, home again." Faith slung her backpack over one shoulder and scooped up Watson. She kissed her aunt good-bye, then went to unlock her bicycle from the rack out front. She was glad Watson didn't balk at being back in the basket, not that she would have blamed him if he had after their wild trip into town. As she wheeled away from the library, she couldn't help looking over her shoulder toward the corner of the building. Giving in to curiosity, she changed direction and walked the bike around the corner. "Short detour, Watson," she said. "Let's get a good look at these after-hours pickup boxes."

The boxes were set into the library's east wall near the drive-up book return. They worked very much like post office boxes, with access doors inside the library for staff and outside for patrons who weren't able to pick up materials when the library was open. Faith wondered if setting the boxes into the wall had been controversial when it was done. It had meant putting a hole in the side of the historic building. But the work had been done beautifully, and the design of the whole fixture fit the looks of the building.

"There's a light so people can see what they're doing with the keypad after dark. But if I remember right, it's only just bright enough for the keys, so I don't know if we'd be able to see the kidnapper's face with it."

Watson leaped out of the basket and went to sniff along the base of the wall while Faith studied the side of the building some more. She didn't see any security cameras. She slowly pivoted on the spot. She didn't see any places nearby where anyone could hide and watch the pickup boxes. From her limited experience, Faith knew there wasn't much nightlife in Lighthouse Bay. So chances were good that someone wearing dark clothes and a hat or a hood wouldn't be seen by anyone in the wee hours of the morning. She turned and studied the building again. One of the second-floor windows, right about where the mystery section was, should have a clear view of the drive-up lane and the pickup boxes.

The cat didn't like seeing his human unhappy. She'd been unhappy since the woman named Charlotte left their meeting. Now she was pensive as well as unhappy. Pensive was okay. Pensive was the natural demeanor of intelligent cats. But his human's unhappiness was hard to bear. It was a kind of unhappiness he'd seen before, the kind that rubbing fur around her ankles never entirely eased. He wasn't one to give up, though, so he applied himself and his fur to her ankles with vigor. She barely noticed. Luckily the place to get delicious, crunchy fish things was across the street. Stopping there always put a purr in her voice. In his too. He headed off in that direction, knowing she would follow.

"Hey," Faith called. "Where are you running off to?" Faith caught up to Watson at Happy Tails across the street from the library. The business was Midge's brainchild. The shop carried treats for cats, dogs, and horses, and featured favorites like Strawberry Pupcakes and Cranberry Mutt Bread.

"I should've known you were headed here," Faith said. "Hold on a minute." She locked the bike to a rack in front of the store and then held the door for Watson. "Hi, Sarah," she said with a wave to the shop's manager behind the counter.

"Hi there, Watson," Sarah said. "Oh, and hi to you too, Faith. I didn't see you at first. I only had eyes for him." It was the kind of joke Sarah Goodwin never got tired of. She knew the names of most pets in Lighthouse Bay and quickly learned the names of visitors' pets, endearing herself to the humans who arrived with her customers.

"This guy thinks he deserves a treat," Faith said. "And I agree."

"Rough day?" Sarah asked.

"Not smooth, anyway." Faith asked for a small bag of the Tunaroons and another of the Shrimp Whiskers. The tuna-flavored macaroons were Watson's favorite treats, but he also enjoyed the seafood version of cheese straws. Faith gave a sample of each to him and then tucked the bags into her backpack. If she put them in the bike basket with Watson, they'd be gone before she'd pedaled to the end of the block. "See you, Sarah."

When they stepped out of the shop, Faith heard a car horn. Brooke and her red Miata sat at the curb.

"Hey, you two, Eileen said you might like a ride back. Hop in."

"I've got my bike."

"Midge said she'll bring it out later when she picks up Atticus and Sir Arfer. Leave your bike key with Sarah."

"Is this a conspiracy?"

"Of course."

"Well, what do you think, Watson?" Faith looked around her feet for the cat, then saw him sitting in the Miata's passenger seat. "That answers that. Be right back." She left her bike key with Sarah, and then she plucked Watson from the seat. "In my arms the whole way, buster. Take it easy on the curves, will you, Brooke?"

"Aye aye, captain."

"Did you find your time travel romance?"

"I sure did. I'll let you know if I think we should read it for book club." Brooke suggested steamy romance novels for the group with predictable regularity.

"Somehow I don't see Aunt Eileen going along with it."

"I live in hope."

"Why is Midge taking Sir Arfer home with her?"

"Now that she knows what's going on, she thinks it might be a good idea to keep him at her place until Gloria is back."

"That makes sense."

"Did Charlotte's decision get you down?"

"Hmm?"

"You're not your usual bubbly, sunny self," Brooke said. "You can still ask questions, you know. It's kind of part of who you are."

"Is that a good thing?"

"That doesn't count as a question."

"Okay. What do you think of Lindsey? What do you know about her?"

Brooke scrunched her nose. "Really? Lindsey?" She shrugged a shoulder. "Her last name's Hannah. She's new at the manor. Sweet. Quiet. My angelfish trust her, and I've never known them to steer me wrong."

The cat listened to the words of the humans. He'd never trusted a fish farther than he could catch it and eat it, and so he thought they should be cautious of this assessment. He wrinkled his nose in derision.

"Did you just sneeze, Watson?" Faith asked. She hoped that with everything else, he wasn't coming down with a cold. *What if he ran into something he's allergic to in the woods? Like the invasive honeysuckle?*

"Lindsey's car needs to have some work done on it," Brooke said. "A few times she hasn't been able to get to work. But she does what she can, including borrowing a car to get there. A couple of times she's spent the night so she didn't have to worry. Of course, then she worries about her family. But I'd say all of that is proof of a good work ethic."

"What color is it?"

"Work ethics have colors?" Brooke asked.

"Sorry. I meant Lindsey's car."

"One of those non-color colors. Grayish maybe?"

Brooke pulled up in front of the cottage. Faith thanked her and got out.

"My advice?" Brooke said. "Read a good mystery and see if you can solve it before the sleuth. It's a substitute for the real thing, but substitutes are a lot less messy."

Supper in front of the fireplace in her cottage sounded just right that evening. The comfort of a toasted cheese sandwich and a cup of tomato soup might also help put her in a better frame of mind. She laid kindling and a few pieces of split maple on the grate, then put a match to them. Watson joined her for supper in front of the fire, with the promise of a few Tunaroons and Shrimp Whiskers for dessert.

While Faith ate, she went over the next day's schedule. She planned to be in the manor library in the morning—what she called her "office hours." Part of her job was making herself available to guests. The highlight of the afternoon was to be her interview with Tanya. She read through her questions again and then asked them aloud to get the rhythm of them, hoping they would sound natural. But the combination of warm food, the crackling fire, and the sleepless night before made it hard to concentrate.

When Watson left his bowl and came to sit with her, she put her notes aside to ponder the question she found much more interesting than where Tanya's ideas for murder weapons came from: How had the kidnapper gotten Gloria away? Faith had seen no signs of a struggle in the suite. Gloria had left nothing behind. The note and envelope—in the lavender color Gloria seemed to love—bore handwriting that might be hers, but Faith had never seen her handwriting, so she had no way to know. No one had mentioned being woken by screams. But if Gloria had been drugged, it would have taken more than one strong person to carry her anywhere, even if they hadn't carried her any farther than a secret passage and a hidden room. So how had the kidnapping been accomplished?

And what would happen now? Had Charlotte really made things simple by saying she'd turn the necklace over? She said Gloria would be released and it would be over. But was that the way these kidnappers worked? What if they just delivered new demands?

Faith looked at Watson. He was sound asleep with his head on her hand. While she watched, his paws twitched, as if he were running in a dream. Her thoughts started wandering in a different direction.

What if Charlotte wasn't really trying to keep it simple? Maybe she was involved in Gloria's disappearance somehow. She could be partners with someone. Was that idea really any more outlandish than thinking Gloria engineered it? But Faith didn't like this line of thinking at all. It was taking her down the path of being disloyal to her employer, a woman she liked and admired. Besides, what would Charlotte get out of kidnapping Gloria?

Faith was glad when the phone interrupted. It was Eileen, too keyed up to say hello.

"The necklace is in the pickup box."

"So it *was* in the manor safe?" Faith asked.

"I felt like a secret agent saying that," Eileen said. "We were more than forty-eight hours ahead of schedule. And yes, thank goodness, the necklace was in the safe."

"Why so soon?" Faith asked. "Wouldn't the necklace have been safer in the safe until closer to the deadline? A lot can happen in two days."

"Charlotte didn't want to wait."

"Do you think that's odd?"

"Under these circumstances, I don't know what's normal. But I do know this: That kidnapper had better hope every part of this operation goes smoothly, because if there's any damage to Gloria or to library property, he or she or they will face the wrath of one very angry, very self-righteous librarian."

Eileen called again the next morning as Faith was leaving the cottage. She told Faith that in the middle of the night, she'd realized she should put a book in the pickup box along with the necklace.

"Otherwise, if the kidnapper is someone who knows how the boxes work, it would be obvious that Charlotte was using the box in an unorthodox way, and the only way she could do that would be to convince me or one of my staff to bend the rules. And then the kidnapper might think she'd let something slip. So I couldn't bear to wait and I came in early to put a book in the box along with the necklace."

"Good idea," Faith said.

"Except that when I opened the pickup box, the necklace was gone." Eileen waited for a reaction from Faith but didn't get one. "Faith? Did you hear me?"

"This means the kidnapper is watching Charlotte more closely than we thought. Did you tell Charlotte?"

"Not yet."

"I'll tell her. She's coming across the lawn toward me right now. At a dead run."

11

"I need to speak with you," Charlotte said. "Now. Inside." She jerked her head toward the former gardener's cottage.

Charlotte was in a state of . . . was it controlled hysteria? Those were the only words that came to Faith's mind. There was no flicker of Charlotte's usual perfect smile. Her voice sounded tight enough to crack. Despite running across the lawn, she wasn't breathing hard, and although she gazed steadily at Faith, she startled at a crow flapping out of the Victorian garden. She must have seen the phone at Faith's ear, but she didn't seem to care. She didn't appear to be unsteady, but she put out her hand as if to take Faith's arm. To pull her to the cottage? On instinct, Faith put up her free hand and took a step back. She wondered if she was operating in her own odd state—controlled paranoia?

"I'm on the phone with Aunt Eileen, Charlotte." Faith pointed at the phone and spoke so that both Eileen and Charlotte heard. "Aunt Eileen, Charlotte's anxious to talk to me. Charlotte, if you don't mind, shall we go to the manor library? We'll make sure we're alone there before we talk." There they would be alone in a building full of people rather than alone and away from everyone.

"Let her know what happened," Eileen said.

"I will. And I'll call you back in ten or fifteen minutes."

Faith didn't think she had any real reason to be afraid of Charlotte, but with so many unusual things happening, why take chances? There was something about the way Charlotte was acting that worried her, but she still couldn't identify the reason.

Fortunately, Charlotte seemed willing to go with her, and they crossed the lawn. Watson met them on the terrace.

"Ready for work?" Faith asked him. She unlocked one of the library's French doors and ushered Charlotte and Watson inside. Watson immediately started the hard work of settling for a nap in a pool of sunlight.

Unlike the Candle House Library, there were no official library hours at Castleton Manor. As soon as she and Charlotte were inside, Faith did a quick walk-through, scanning the second-floor balcony and looking in all the favorite reading nooks. There wasn't anything she could do about secret passages or hidden spaces, but she could at least try to make sure they were alone. Satisfied, she checked the time. On Tuesday mornings she liked to be available to guests between nine and noon. It was only eight thirty. Plenty of time to find out why Charlotte wanted to see her.

Charlotte had chosen a seat at the end of the library least visible from any of the doorways. She sat on the edge of the chair, looking uncomfortable and impatient.

On edge is right, Faith thought. *She looks like Watson when he knows we aren't making a social call to the vet.* She was also aware of Charlotte watching her. She didn't know Charlotte quite well enough to know what she might be thinking, but it dawned on her that Charlotte was uneasy because of *her*. She chose a chair near Charlotte where she could see the doors. Then she made a point of relaxing her shoulders and laying her hands loosely in her lap. If she appeared to be relaxed, maybe that would help Charlotte relax.

It didn't.

With a shaking hand, Charlotte showed Faith another lavender envelope. Like the first envelope, it had Charlotte's name written on it. "Slipped under my door," Charlotte said.

"On the third floor?" Faith knew that guests didn't have access to the family quarters on the third floor.

"And the writing looks the same," Charlotte said. "It looks like Gloria's handwriting. Just the way she's written my name when she's signed books for me."

"Do you have any of those books here at Castleton?" Faith asked.

"Yes, in the library upstairs." She was referring to the private family library, also on the third floor.

Gloria has signed enough books that it wouldn't be hard to find her signature, but someone who can get up to the third floor to put a note under Charlotte's door could also get into the library to copy that signature. "What time did you go to bed last night, and what time did you find the envelope?" Faith asked.

"Yesterday was exhausting," Charlotte said. "I was in bed before ten. But I didn't sleep well and I was up by six. I decided to go for an early walk on the beach. I love watching the sunrise. But then I found this."

If she got up at six, what has she been doing all this time? Faith was glad she'd spent time the evening before practicing follow-up questions. This was a different kind of interview, though. Now she needed to avoid asking leading questions. "Did you hear anything last night?"

Charlotte shook her head. Faith was disappointed, but she figured that had been too much to hope for. She doubted there were squeaking floorboards anywhere in the manor, but a muted conversation in the hall or a suspicious rattle of the doorknob would have been nice.

"It would be good to know how late Wolfe stayed up and if he heard anything," Faith said. "Have you spoken to him this morning?"

"No."

"Have you read the letter?"

"I did." Charlotte's words were at odds with her shaking head. "But I don't understand. I don't understand it." Once she'd started shaking her head, she seemed unable to stop.

"Charlotte?" Faith said, trying to get her attention. "What don't you understand?" She reached over and touched Charlotte's arm.

Charlotte jumped, but she held the envelope out to Faith.

"Wait a sec. I'll be right back." Faith went to the drawer where she kept the cotton gloves for handling fragile and rare books. She put on a pair, then accepted the envelope from Charlotte and slipped the note out. It was another ransom note with ugly threats similar to those in the first one. "The first line is despicable."

"There's nothing about a ransom note that isn't," Charlotte said.

"You're right." Faith read the rest of the note.

But wait, there's more! Deliver Grimm's Fairy Tales *by Michael Patrick to hold box 3. Use combination 1004. Do not go to the police. Do not tell anyone. Do not try to find Gloria. Do this by midnight Wednesday. Follow these instructions exactly. Gloria remains safe. But only if you follow my instructions. If you do not, the world will never read another new book by Gloria Bauer. That's a promise. You are being watched.*

"Is the kidnapper trying to be funny with that first line?" Faith asked. "Does he think he's playing a game?"

"That's part of what I don't understand," Charlotte said. "Is this all a sick joke to someone? Is Gloria really missing? Is *she* behind it?"

"What else don't you understand about the note?"

"The deadline is tomorrow night. They're asking for the book before they've taken the necklace. That doesn't make sense. Unless they're going to keep asking for more and more."

"Unfortunately, I think that's the way some kidnappers work." Faith knew she needed to tell Charlotte that the kidnapper had already picked up the necklace, but she wanted an answer first. "Charlotte, why come to me this morning? Why show me the note? Yesterday you were clear that you didn't want anyone else involved. Because of the danger, you said. But today the stakes are higher. The same threats, the same deadline, but another demand. Why the change?"

"I spoke with Wolfe last night."

"About this? About Gloria?" *Was that a good idea?* Faith wondered. *But why wouldn't it be?*

"About you."

That answer stopped Faith's thoughts in their tracks. She wasn't sure what to think of it or how to react. She looked over at Watson. He lay on his back in his puddle of sunshine, in no hurry to do anything else. *That's the idea. Wait patiently.* As calm as a cat, she looked at Charlotte and waited for her to continue or explain. Unfortunately, Charlotte seemed to be waiting too, and Faith began to feel like she was being examined with a magnifying glass. She struggled not to tug on her skirt or pat her hair.

"He trusts you," Charlotte finally said. "He says you're cool and calm, and I can see that you are. He also says you're intelligent and you don't take stupid chances."

"That's—"

"Kind of him? I told him to be careful about sounding patronizing."

Faith suppressed a smile. "You didn't tell him about Gloria?"

"No. He often won't take chances, stupid or otherwise. In this situation, I think he would go straight to the police."

"Maybe we should," Faith said. She didn't want to play devil's advocate, but it was important to find out exactly how Charlotte felt. "Maybe we're playing with Gloria's life."

"Not as long as the kidnapper wants something," Charlotte said. "Or wants something more."

"What if she's already dead? What if it's too late to rescue her?"

"Then it's also too late for the police to rescue her," Charlotte said. She spoke firmly, but Faith saw the color drain from her face as she made the bald statement.

Faith wondered about a woman who acted as though she was near panic one minute and running a boardroom meeting the next. But maybe she needed to give Charlotte points for pulling herself together in the midst of a situation for which she had no blueprint or business plan. The outcome of this "situation" might have a very real effect on the future of Castleton Manor, and it was time to tell her about the necklace.

"There's something I need to tell you," Faith said. "There's been another development."

Faith looked at the time again—Aunt Eileen would be expecting her call in a few minutes. She opened the locked bookcase. She and Charlotte both looked over their shoulders when she did.

"I'm glad I'm not the only one who's feeling eyes everywhere," Charlotte said. Then Faith wrapped the precious *Grimm's Fairy Tales* in acid-free tissue she kept in the drawer with the cotton gloves and handed it to Charlotte. She worried Charlotte might sob as Faith handed it to her.

"What do they want with one book?" Charlotte said. "One book is valuable, but not nearly what it would be worth as part of the set."

Faith could think of a few reasons for breaking up a set, the first being to *ruin* the value of it for the owner—Castleton Manor. Or ultimately, the Jaxons. She didn't think Charlotte needed to hear that possibility from her. Charlotte's imagination seemed to be giving her enough problems.

But another reason to take one book from the set might be to add value by completing another. Patrick had produced only three of his folk- and fairy-tale sets. Castleton Manor owned two. Who owned the third? Or half of the third set? Faith didn't know, but maybe she could find out.

"Here," Charlotte said. She pulled a small manila envelope from her purse and held it out.

Faith almost dropped the envelope when she realized the ransom notes were inside.

"I want you to keep them. I can't bear to see them or have them near me anymore."

"I'll, uh, I'll keep them safe," Faith said. "And I'll call Aunt Eileen and tell her you're on your way."

"Please tell her about that wretched second note, will you? I can't bear to discuss them anymore, either. Will you call another meeting of the book club?"

"I'll be in contact with the others, but we probably can't all get away from work on short notice. So no, we won't meet."

"But what do you plan to do?" Charlotte asked. Her mind seemed to have left the organization of the boardroom behind and she was back to being rattled.

"I'll do what I do best—look for information."

"What do you hope to find?" Charlotte sounded almost

fretful and cradled the tissue-wrapped book in her arms the way Faith had cradled Watson the day before.

"Are you going to be all right?" Faith asked her.

Charlotte assured her she would and Faith walked with her to the door. She was glad Charlotte didn't ask again what Faith hoped to find. *Clues? Suspects? A kidnapper?* What she hoped to find was any crumb of information that would lead her down the right path—to find Gloria and foil the kidnapper. She just hoped she'd know the right path when she saw it.

"What are you going to do?" Eileen asked when Faith dropped the bombshell of the second ransom note and told her to expect Charlotte with the book.

That question again. But she knew Eileen would understand the piecemeal nature of her information gathering. "What's the best way to find out who owns books made by Michael Patrick? Books and other artwork. Who owns or who might be looking to own?"

"Like so many good questions, that one keeps getting bigger," Eileen said. "Some of the books might actually be listed in an online database I found. I read recently that more than seventy thousand libraries are now searchable through it, but given the value and rarity of Patrick's books, it's unlikely anyone who has one will lend it. There might be articles online that'll give you clues. There used to be a weekly journal called *AB Bookman's Weekly.* Before the Internet, it was the best place to find or sell used, rare, and antique books. It was a little gold mine in your mailbox every week, with long lists of books wanted and for sale and themed reference lists."

"Not published anymore?" Faith asked.

"No, but do you know where I saw stacks of old issues? The Fishwife's Attic, the antiques shop down past the hardware store. Corrie Baker owns the shop. She has a little bit of everything, and way more old magazines and journals than she'll ever sell. She has them stacked around the walls upstairs. They're probably good insulation."

"Were they ever indexed?" Faith asked, thinking the project sounded like looking for a needle in a haystack.

"I want to say yes, semiannually, but I might be thinking of some other journal."

"Huh. I guess I'll try to get over there. If nothing else, maybe Corrie knows something about Patrick. In the meantime, I want to get another look at Gloria's suite. Then, if I don't get too many interruptions this morning, I'll study the two notes and try to figure out what else they might tell us."

"What they tell us is be careful in everything you do," Eileen said. "But of course I know you will be."

"Tanya mentioned a Patrick retrospective in Provincetown a few years back. She said there weren't any books, but that gallery might be able to tell us something."

"Why don't I tackle the online search for Patrick?" Eileen said. "I'll check out your Provincetown show. I've got a few other ideas, plus an ace in the hole—one of my grad school classmates is a librarian at Yale. She might be willing to help with an art history database search."

"Fantastic."

"It might not turn anything up."

"Sitting around doing nothing won't turn anything up either,"

Faith said. "I'd like you to look more closely at the notes, if you have time."

"I might be able to run out there this afternoon."

"I'm interviewing Tanya Race at two."

"I'll try to make it," Eileen said. "No promises."

Faith knew where the master keys to the guest suites were kept behind the inn's registration desk. If she was lucky, the clerk would be off on an errand . . .

But when Faith arrived at the desk, the young woman behind it looked up from her tablet and swiped it off. "Caught in the act," she said with a rueful grin.

"It's a quiet morning," Faith said. "I'm sure you're not the first person who ever wanted to get caught up on the news while you have some quiet time."

"The news. Right." The young woman winked. "What can I do for you?"

"I need to check on something in the du Maurier Suite. May I have the key? Oh, and by the way, have you seen Ms. Russell recently?"

"She came by earlier and I saw her get in the elevator. Going down, I think. Would you like me to call her?"

"No, that's okay. But thanks." Faith hoped the clerk was right. The idea of Marlene catching her in a guest suite made her nervous.

The clerk handed Faith the key. Faith thanked her again and ran up the stairs.

There was no one leaving Gloria's suite this morning as Faith approached. Still "feeling eyes everywhere," as Charlotte had said,

Faith couldn't help looking over her shoulder before unlocking the door. But when she went in, she knew immediately she was too late.

The du Maurier Suite smelled of liberally applied furniture polish. She saw the pattern left by the vacuum cleaner on the carpet. There was no hint of the lavender she'd smelled the morning before in the bathroom, only the astringency of disinfectant. On the desk in the sitting room was a tent card, welcoming a future guest to the suite, signed by the person who'd cleaned the room so thoroughly. It read *Lindsey* in looping purple letters.

Faith picked the tent card up, touching only its edges, and put it with the ransom notes in her backpack. She listened at the suite door but didn't hear anyone. She swung it open and came face-to-face with Rachel Vail.

"Leaving the scene of the crime?" Rachel asked.

12

"Rachel, good to see you." Faith pulled the suite door shut behind her. *And let me pull my heart out of my throat.* "Sorry, I missed what you said when I opened the door."

"Just wondering if this was the room where the great Gloria was staying. You wouldn't catch me running off in the night if I'd just won the Mary Stewart award and been given the du Maurier Suite. I'm guessing it's posh, right? And paid for? But even if she didn't get it *gratis*, she wouldn't have had to scrape her pennies together to stay here."

"Is there anything I can do for you, Rachel?"

"Give me a tour?" Rachel pointed over Faith's head at the suite's door.

"It's a beautiful suite," Faith said, "and I know it sounds like a refrain, but giving a tour of it isn't my call. Ask Marlene."

Faith wished for and received a quiet morning in the library. She helped a woman find the title of a favorite book from her childhood and showed another the library's collection of vintage knitting patterns. She had time to text Brooke and Midge to let them know about developments. She received appropriately shocked texts in return. But when Tanya came in and asked for visiting privileges with the *Grimm's Fairy Tales*, she realized she was in trouble. She hadn't planned for how to explain the book's absence. Neither had Charlotte.

"Unfortunately, Charlotte Jaxon borrowed it this morning," Faith told Tanya. "A special request. I don't usually let it out of my sight, much less the library."

"But she owns the book and the business. And therefore your job." Tanya tried to smile her way past the dig. "I wanted to see his Rumpelstiltskin." She tapped her foot, then pointed at Faith. "You said you have two sets."

"We do, but the second set is in very fragile condition. Every time a page is turned in one of the books, part of it crumbles. I'm sorry. I can let you know when the first one's back. Or would you like to see one of the other Patrick volumes? Scottish fairy tales? American tall tales?"

"No, never mind. The interview's at two, right? See you then."

"Wait—did you want to meet ahead of time to go over the questions?"

"Winging it works better," Tanya said. "Keeps the answers fresh. I've probably heard all your questions before anyway."

Faith stared at her back as she left and saw Brooke stand aside at the door to let her out.

"Another happy customer," Brooke said, nodding after Tanya. "Books might even be more satisfying than food."

"*She* wasn't satisfied." Faith lowered her voice. "She wanted to look at the *Grimm's*."

"Oh. Well, don't worry about it. She didn't look too upset. Are we alone?"

"Except for Watson."

"What's up, kitty cat?" Brooke asked Watson.

Watson blinked from his favorite chair.

"I'm on break," Brooke said. "Show me what you have. Then I'll tell you who I saw this morning."

Faith unlocked a drawer of her desk. Wearing the cotton gloves, she brought out the notes, envelopes, and tent card and laid them side by side on the desk.

"Extremely creepy," Brooke said after reading the new note. She pointed to the envelopes and the tent card. "Similar handwriting?"

"Similar, but is it really Lindsey's?"

"That's an interesting thought." Brooke almost picked up the tent card but stopped herself and put her hands behind her back. "I'll do some looking and asking."

"Be careful—of her, in case she is involved, but *for* her too. If she isn't involved we don't want to jeopardize her job."

"Anyone who makes the light, airy soufflés I'm known for is guaranteed to have a delicate touch," Brooke said. "Now I'll tell you my news and then scoot. You know I'm doing the baking this week, right? So I get here way early, like pitch-black early. By the time it was light enough to see the edge of the woods, the kitchen was toasty, and I stepped outside to cool off. And there's Jed Knowlan walking out of the woods along the road that goes nowhere. I got the impression he didn't expect anyone to see him. He said he was an early morning runner."

"You don't believe him?

"No. When I cook for people, I notice what they eat. He doesn't look like a runner, he doesn't move like one, and believe me, he doesn't eat like one."

"Was he wearing athletic shoes?" Faith asked.

"You'd think I'd have noticed whether he was. Sherlock Holmes I am not."

"That's okay. Maybe I can sneak a question about exercise into my interview with him on Thursday."

"Something like, 'Tell me, Jed, what's your fastest running time when you're out to snatch a kidnap victim?'"

"Oh yeah, no way he'll catch on to that. Do you know what Gloria said about his writing once? In print? That his books are thrill-less and his characters are thugs."

"Ooh, burn," Brooke said. "Maybe it's a good thing she isn't here." She clapped a hand across her mouth in horror. "Did I really just say that? Sometimes I wonder about your friends, Faith. Honestly. But if Jed isn't a runner, what was the point of telling me he is?"

The salon was a versatile room, not as posh as the Great Hall, but still one of Faith's favorites. She'd seen it used for cooking demonstrations and dance lessons. The next afternoon it would become a movie theater. It was a more intimate space than the Great Hall, so it was perfect for a cozy interview.

Unfortunately, Tanya's preference for "winging it" also seemed to mean she didn't like showing up until her audience was seated and the interviewer was getting nervous. But she arrived in the salon unflustered and greeted Faith like an old friend. Only when she sat down and focused on the number of empty chairs in front of her did her smile take on a brittle quality.

"Sorry if I kept you waiting," she said. "I looked in the program guide and saw that Gloria's interview on Friday is in the gallery. You know, that room that's about half a mile from here?" She waited through the audience's laughter. "Silly me, I thought all the interviews would be in that beautiful and very large space. I thought wrong, though, and really shouldn't have. I mean, this should have been my first clue about where I rate in the great scheme of author interviews." She held up her Simmering Suspense Week program guide for the audience to see and pointed first to Gloria's smiling face taking up the entire inside cover and then to the smaller photos of herself and Jed on the opposite page.

Alyssa, sitting in the middle of the front row, said, "Oh no no. We think you're just as important."

"She's right," Jed called from the audience. "Size doesn't always matter. Besides, the only clue you needed was actually reading the schedule. Your interview is first, after all."

Tanya laughed with the audience. When the laughter died, she held up Gloria's picture again. "But don't you love this picture? I've been seeing it on her book jackets for so many years and never get tired of it. That braid on top of her head, the smile—classic Gloria. A classy lady. I know we're all missing her this week."

"Thank you, Tanya. A nice tribute," Faith said, finding it hard not to grit her teeth. "And now, ladies and gentlemen, welcome to our afternoon interview with another classy lady, Tanya Race. Let's get started, shall we? Where do you—"

"Wait, wait," Tanya said. "Let me guess. Actually, do you know what we could do? It might be fun. You ask the first half of a question. I'll try to guess the second half and then I'll answer based on my guess. What do you think? No?"

"Well, it's your interview. If you want—"

"No, you're right. We'll do it your way. But you were going to ask where I get my ideas from, right?"

Faith smiled. "Actually, it was where do you see yourself in five years? But your question is great, so go right ahead."

"I like yours better," Tanya said. "Best-seller lists nationwide."

Faith took a deep breath while the audience laughed again. She considered throwing her notes over her shoulder and turning the stage over to Tanya. But after the audience settled down again, Tanya surprised her by settling back and taking the interview seriously.

She was candid about wanting to quit her day job and write full time, and about how hard it could be for someone who's happy spending so much time alone with the characters in her head to then come out and be social with real people. She told the audience she felt lucky because she liked the social parts of writing as much as being solitary. She listened to Faith's questions as if each was new and required careful thought. Her answers came easily and sounded insightful. But Tanya's answers had a way of circling back around to make little digs at Gloria, along with a few at Jed, though Faith watched him laugh those off. But the digs at Gloria bothered her, and from Jed's reaction, they bothered him too.

"Tanya, thank you. You've been very open with us. We have time for a couple more questions. You said you enjoy the social parts of writing, and we've seen ample evidence of that here this afternoon. What's been one of your best experiences out meeting your public?"

"Faith, that's what I call a 'hero question.' Heroes are never as interesting as bad guys. So I'm going to answer the bad guy version and tell you about my worst experience. I was asked to do a signing at a bookstore, which shall remain nameless. I was flattered. I jumped at it, because if you're trying to make it, you have to, right? I got there—and I wanted to cry. Because despite its bookish name, which is appropriate in a depressing way, this business wasn't much more than an outlet for books remaindered by their publishers—'remaindered' meaning they were books that not enough people wanted in the first place, so they'd been trucked there. Generally speaking, when you're looking at a book in this 'bookstore,' you're seeing it in its grave. And my first two books were there front and center."

There was a single muffled cough in the audience. Faith thought it might be Jed, but she couldn't be sure.

"All right, so that was a downer," Tanya said. "Sorry. But thank you for showing respect for those books with your moment of silence." She turned to Faith. "Now ask me something fun so we can end on a high note."

"Um . . . okay, if you were going to be stranded on a desert island and you could choose one person to be stranded with you, would you choose—"

"The guy with the inflatable boat in his back pocket."

"Would you choose Prince Charming or Rumpelstiltskin?"

There was another single muffled cough in the audience while Tanya stared at Faith. Then Tanya asked, "What kind of question is that? Uh-uh. My first answer stands. Thank you, Faith. Thanks, everyone. All ten or twelve of you. Refreshments are ready in the back of the room."

Faith once again felt like throwing her notes over her shoulder. She wasn't sure she should feel any better when Heath Westcott gave her a thumbs-up on his way out.

Eileen called after the interview. "I'm sorry I missed it."

"Ugh. Don't be."

"What happened?"

"Let's just say interviewing strong personalities isn't one of my strengths."

"It probably wasn't as bad as you think. These things usually aren't. I'm sorry it felt rough. And I'm sorry that I won't be able to get out there at all today. Seth called in sick, which actually has had a silver lining. Tuesday afternoons are quiet here, so between patrons I had time to spend hunting Michael Patrick."

"Any luck?"

"I spoke to the gallery owner in Provincetown. She's very enthusiastic. She made me wish I'd seen the Michael Patrick retrospective, and she was excited to learn about the Patrick books at the manor. She said they put together their own small version of a gallery guide for their show. She's putting one in the mail to you for the library, but in the meantime she'll scan her copy and e-mail the pages to me."

"That's wonderful."

"It'll probably be a dead end," Eileen said, "but now you'll know someone with more than a passing interest in Michael Patrick, and you'll get a reference work for your library's collection out of it. What about Gloria's suite? Any luck there?"

"Just more questions." Faith told her about the spotless room and the cleaning card with Lindsey's name on it. "I have the card. I'd like to compare it with something else that I know for sure has her signature, even if just to rule it out."

"Why would anyone forge Lindsey's name on a cleaning card?"

"For that matter," Faith said, "if Lindsey's involved, why would she take a chance and write Charlotte's name on the envelope herself? And have you noticed that every time we find something we think might be a clue and then look at it more closely, it ends up looking exactly like a mare's nest?"

"That might be the nature of investigations," Eileen said. "Think of it like a jigsaw puzzle. They're a total jumble at the beginning. And working my way through what looks like a hopeless tangle is certainly how many of my knitting projects start out. It might help to list what we know or what we think we know about the kidnapper. Like taking an inventory of supplies before starting a long journey."

"That's kind of poetic, Aunt Eileen."

"I've been reading the journal of a Pack Horse Librarian who traveled in the Appalachians at the turn of the last century. Amazing woman. She planned her trips meticulously. All right, I'll start. The kidnapper, or someone associated with the kidnapper, obviously has insider knowledge. Proof? Choosing the after-hours pickup boxes. That tells us this person is at least somewhat familiar with the library, and by extension, Lighthouse Bay. *But* he calls it a 'hold box' in the letters. They *are* hold boxes, but we don't call them that and never have. So this is a person who's familiar with us but not entirely familiar."

"Someone with insider knowledge and insider access," Faith said. "Someone able to get up to the third floor of the manor. This is useful, Aunt Eileen." She scribbled notes while they talked. "What else do we know?"

"He has current information. He sent the note to Charlotte. More often than not, she's on Martha's Vineyard and not here. But he knows she's here this week. And that makes me worry about what he knows or what he's finding out. And . . . that's really all I've got. Are you being safe?"

"Always, Aunt Eileen. Watson and I are spending another exciting evening behind our locked doors and windows, eating supper in front of the fire and coming up with interview questions for Jed." To save her aunt worry, Faith didn't tell her what she and Midge were going to do *before* supper.

The cat didn't visit the beach as often as he would have liked. He enjoyed the wide variety of briny smells found near the water, but he didn't enjoy the gulls. Laughing gulls were especially annoying, even if they weren't laughing at anyone in particular, as he'd heard his human say. Late that afternoon, he welcomed the opportunity to beachcomb in the company of his human and her friend who smelled like a confused mixture of Tunaroons and rabies vaccinations. They also brought the yapper they called Sir Arfer. The humans thought they were conducting an experiment with the dog. They hoped that by taking him for a walk on the beach near where he'd been found, he might follow his own trail back to where he'd come from. The cat hoped the experiment would succeed and the dog would go back to where he came from, but he could not help being a realist. He knew that his wish and the humans' experiment were both hopeless. The yapper's attention span wasn't up to the challenge.

"Anyway, it was a nice walk," his human said.

"I'll take him back home." The other woman shook her head over the dog still prancing around her feet. "He went nowhere and everywhere and all of it fast."

"He's kind of a ditz, isn't he? At least we learned that."

Hearing his human's conclusion, the cat reassessed his opinion of the beach experiment. If learning that piece of information had been its aim, then it was clearly a resounding success.

An hour before Faith wanted to be up the next morning, her phone chirped with an incoming text. She hadn't silenced it, just in case. She groped for it, then squinted at a message from Midge: *Bad news. Break-in. Sir Arfer gone.*

In one fluid movement, Faith sat up, flipped on her reading lamp, and dialed Midge, who answered before Faith's eyes adjusted to the lamp.

"'Gone' as in got out?" Faith asked.

"'Gone' as in taken. The other animals were all worked up, and his kennel looks like it was forced open. Sorry if I woke you." Midge was breathing hard.

"Are you and Peter all right? The other animals?"

"We are fine. Peter called the police. I let him do all the talking. He doesn't know about Gloria. I feel terrible." Midge disconnected.

Seconds later, Faith's phone rang.

"Maybe it *is* Gloria," Midge said. "Maybe she *did* arrange all this. And then the dog ran off, but she couldn't run after him because she was in hiding, and then when she figured out he was here, she sneaked in and got him back."

"I can't quite picture her skulking around and stealing her own dog."

"Yeah, you're right. But Sir Arfer *did* run off from somewhere. It's a long shot, but I'm going to drive around areas where I know there are empty houses near the beach and look for anything suspicious. See if I can figure out where Gloria might be. I'll do it when I'm out on house calls. I feel awful."

"You know this isn't your fault," Faith said. "And this time of year there are a lot of empty houses. For that matter, it might not be an empty house."

"But this is something I can do," Midge said. "And I *do* feel terrible."

"You're a good friend, Midge. Please be careful."

Faith's phone rang again while she and Watson were having breakfast.

"I'm getting leery about answering phones, Watson."

She saw Watson run his tongue over his lips, probably to get the last precious crumbs of Tunaroon Faith had tipped into his bowl with his kibble. Faith took a sip of coffee and a deep breath and greeted her aunt.

Eileen answered with one word. "Again."

13

Faith's stomach fell into her toes. "'Again' what, Aunt Eileen?"

"It's happened again. The deadline isn't until tonight and the book is already gone. We should have known that might happen and we should've been on stakeout last night. Why weren't we?"

"Because we didn't anticipate an early pickup? And because we're amateurs?" Faith asked.

"Then why haven't we called the police?"

"Because Charlotte asked us not to. Because of the threats to Gloria. I wonder if Charlotte's received another note."

"Do we call her or wait for her to call us?" Eileen asked. "And what if she hasn't? What if we don't hear from the kidnapper again?"

"I think we will." Faith told Eileen about Sir Arfer being stolen.

"Dognapped," Eileen said. "Now we have dognapping."

"That's why I think we'll hear from the kidnapper again. I'll bet Sir Arfer and Gloria were taken together the first time. He got away. Now they've taken him again. What if they took him for Gloria's sake? It would mean she's still alive and there's still hope."

"A kidnapper with a heart of gold?"

"A soft spot for dogs, anyway," Faith said.

"What if it started even earlier—on the night of the reception, when Sir Arfer ran out of the manor? Do you remember that? We heard a yip and he scrambled past us. Was that a first attempt at dognapping?"

"Maybe. Maybe the kidnapper planned to take the dog and use him to lure Gloria. Maybe he *did* take the dog and lure Gloria."

"We need to let Charlotte know about the book and the dog," Eileen said. "Why don't I do that? I know she appreciates all you're doing, and she's holding up well, but hearing this from an old friend might be more bearable."

"Thank you, Aunt Eileen. I was dreading that. I'll update Brooke and Midge."

"This is all so awful. I wish I could come out there this afternoon," Eileen said. "I'd bring my laptop and call it community outreach. Are you interviewing Jed?"

"No, it's movie day. They're serving clam chowder tonight from a scene in Gloria's *Murder With a Splash of Larceny* so they're showing the made-for-TV version of the book this afternoon. Thank goodness I can skip it. How's that for a bad attitude?"

"Don't be so hard on yourself. Is there anything else I can do to help?"

"Pray we *do* hear from the kidnapper again. Because if we don't, I'll worry about what that means."

"I'd rather pray that Gloria and Sir Arfer are released unharmed."

Faith didn't ordinarily have trouble concentrating on her work at the library. There was always a question to answer or a task to perform. The variety and her love of everything about books usually made her days go by as though she'd riffled through their pages to reach the end. But after she finalized her questions for the interview with Jed and with no programming obligation that afternoon, she felt the need to do something more than worry about Gloria and wait to hear from the kidnapper.

She put a note on her desk in the library saying that she'd return in an hour, ran back to the cottage for her car, and went to find The Fishwife's Attic. Parking could sometimes be a problem in Lighthouse Bay, which was one of the reasons she liked riding her bike. But driving made sense today so she'd have more time in the antiques shop without being gone from work too long. Driving had nothing to do with staying safe from careening grayish cars on that winding stretch of road. Or so she insisted to herself.

Eileen had said the shop was down from the hardware store. Now where was the hardware store? If she remembered right, it was around the corner from the post office. She turned there and saw signs for Peterson Brothers Hardware and The Fishwife's Attic on her right. Even better, there were several empty parking spots down a bit farther on the left. Two of the spots had disappeared by the time she was able to turn and come back toward them, but she nabbed the last one and felt victorious. As she got out of her car, she saw Rachel coming out of the antiques shop and ducked down. *Coward. Are you also going to pretend to tie your shoe?* Annoyed with herself, she straightened. Rachel was nowhere to be seen. Her victorious feeling replaced by guilt, she crossed the street.

The Fishwife's Attic was a trove—that much was obvious to Faith as soon as she opened the door. The shop smelled of furniture polish with a hint of dust hidden away in joints and seams. It also smelled of fresh coffee, and Faith's nose pointed her to the source—a mug in the hands of the woman at the sales desk. The woman blew on the steaming mug and raised a hand in greeting.

"Are you Corrie?" Faith asked.

The woman—Corrie—nodded. Without putting the mug down, she picked up a sheet of paper and held it out. Faith skirted a slant-front school desk and a display of hand tools to take the paper.

"Map," Corrie said in a scratchy voice. Then she pointed to her throat. "Strep."

Faith put a hand to her own throat and grimaced her sympathy. "I've got two questions, and you can probably nod or shake your head for each. Eileen Piper told me you have old issues of *AB Bookman's Weekly*."

Corrie nodded, pointed toward the ceiling, and gestured for the map. She pointed to a room to the left of the stairs and circled her finger around the perimeter.

"Do you have any artwork—"

Corrie shook her head before Faith finished her question.

"Anything at all to do with Michael Patrick? He was an illustrator from Truro."

Corrie cocked her head.

"Letters, photographs, books, magazine or newspaper articles . . ." Faith watched Corrie as she listed anything she could think of that might be hidden away in this "attic." Corrie shook her head at all of it. "But what was this for?" Faith asked, mimicking Corrie's cocked head. "You looked confused by it. Sorry. That's not a yes-or-no question."

Corrie held up a finger. Then she opened her eyes wide and gazed around the shop, letting her mouth fall open enough to show wonder.

"Other people looking?" Faith asked.

Corrie pointed at Faith and mouthed "Bingo." Then she puzzled Faith by pointing toward the door.

Faith turned and looked. *Nothing unusual. Oh.* "Do you mean the woman who left just before I came in was asking?"

Corrie gave her a thumbs-up.

"Anyone else? Sorry, not a yes-or-no. How about this? Do you search for items customers are looking for?"

A nod.

"Has anyone been looking for Patrick materials? Specifically the books he made?"

Corrie's face went from open to guarded.

"Can you tell me who?"

Corrie's face closed off completely.

"I take it you believe in patron confidentiality," Faith said.

Corrie started to laugh and ended up in a coughing fit. Faith apologized, moving out of range, she hoped. Then she followed her store map to the stairs. On her way up them, her phone sounded with a text from Brooke: *Lindsey's husband Dillon Hannah works at Lighthouse Cycle and Recycle.*

Faith knew where that was. The shop sold bicycles, rented them to tourists, repaired them, and sold parts. She'd noted the location in case she ever needed them. *And today's as good a time as any to buy a patch kit.*

She followed the map to the room labeled *Misc. Journals* where she was faced with more stacks of magazines than she'd ever seen. Stacks and stacks and stacks.

"Oh dear."

Not all the stacks were neat or orderly. Some had obviously been "shopped." But *AB Bookman's Weekly*, apparently not in high demand, was stacked in four neat columns against a wall. After scanning spines for anything that looked like an annual index and flipping through several issues, Faith realized the futility of this quest. The most recent issue she saw had landed in someone's mailbox in 1994.

How did I think this was going to help?

As she passed through the front room, Faith saw Corrie handing a map to another customer. She'd planned on waving and heading straight for the door but decided to swing by the sales desk. She hung back until the new customer moved off into another room, then stepped up close.

"I'll come back when I have more time," Faith said. "I've got one more non-yes-or-no question. If you won't tell me who's been looking for Michael Patrick material because of confidentiality, then why did you tell me the woman who'd just left asked about them?"

Corrie shrugged and then croaked, "Tourist. I don't know her, so no worries about divulging a name."

Faith thanked her and left, wondering when Corrie would realize her mistake—just because Corrie didn't know who Rachel was didn't mean Faith didn't. Or maybe Corrie didn't feel the need to protect tourists the way she protected people whose names she knew.

Lighthouse Cycle and Recycle was only a few blocks away, so Faith left the car and walked. She took her time, enjoying the shop windows and the smell of someone's wood fire. A few windows still had fake spiderwebs in their corners left over from Halloween. Others were breaking out in cornucopias, Pilgrim hats, and other souvenirs reminding visitors that Cape Cod was the Pilgrims' first landing place before they settled in Plymouth. But when she came to the photography studio's window, she had to stop and admire its parade of holiday efficiency. A scarecrow, a black cat, a turkey, two Pilgrims, a goose, and an elf riding a red-nosed reindeer marched on a bed of maple leaves from a pumpkin on the left to a gingerbread house on the right.

A wide alley separated the photography studio from the bike shop. The businesses had pooled their efforts to turn the space into an inviting courtyard with benches and murals painted on their facing walls. The photography studio's mural was a garden scene with an old-fashioned photographer using a tripod and box camera. The bike shop's mural showed a bicycle race to the lighthouse, with all the bikes being ridden by codfish.

A bell sounded when Faith opened the door at Lighthouse Cycle and Recycle, and a nostalgic smell greeted her. New bicycle tires? She wasn't sure, but as a child it had meant the excitement of getting places under her own wheel power.

A couple of men, probably in their fifties, were discussing a recumbent bike, and one of them waved to let her know he saw her. Another man, young enough to be Dillon Hannah, came out of a back room wiping his hands on a bandanna.

"What can I help you with?" he asked Faith.

"Patch kits?" Faith asked.

The man showed her to the display. She thanked him, glad to see a name tag, but disappointed it said "Aidan." The bell on the door trilled again, and Aidan moved off. She compared kits and wondered how nosy she should be. She picked a kit that was midrange in price, with a patch for every occasion, and carried it to the sales counter. The older man—Travis, according to his name tag—rang her up.

"I can just tuck it in my purse," she said when he reached for a bag. "Is Dillon in?"

"He's not." Travis shut the cash register drawer with a snap that matched the snap of his words.

"That's okay," Faith said. "I work with his wife and just thought I'd say hi, if he was."

"Good mechanic." Travis handed Faith her change. "Quit two weeks ago. Tell Lindsey Travis says hi."

"I will." Faith held up the patch kit. "Thanks."

Faith paused in the courtyard. Maybe she'd misunderstood Brooke's text, so she sent one back: *Lindsey's husband works or worked at bike shop?* She hit Send, looked up, and saw one of the mural's bike-riding codfish move—not so startling when she realized it was painted over the shop's side door. Aidan, the young man she'd first guessed was Dillon, came out and closed the door behind him. He started to light a cigarette but stopped when he noticed her. He glanced over his shoulder at the door, then waved her over.

"Travis is covering for Dillon," he said, cigarette twitching in his hand.

"How do you mean?"

"The two of them go way back. Travis told him he wouldn't let the story get out of how he'd quit. Said he didn't want Lindsey or the kids hurt." Aidan looked over his shoulder at the door again. "Dillon was helping himself to the till. 'Quit' is just a friendly way of saying 'got fired.'"

"Do you know if he's found another job?"

"I wouldn't know. Haven't seen him since he left."

Faith glanced at their surroundings—the courtyard, pretty even on a gray day, but still basically an alley. *And asking loaded questions of strange men in alleys? Is this a good idea?*

"I have to ask. Why are you telling me this? If Travis wants to keep it quiet, why are you telling me, a stranger?"

"Because I'm getting tired of hearing the lie." Aidan dropped the unsmoked cigarette and ground it under his boot. "Because when Travis discovered that money was missing, the first thing good old Dillon did was tell him I stole it."

Now I'm looking at a mare's nest wrapped in a tangle of yarn inside a jigsaw puzzle box, Faith mused on the drive back to Castleton Manor. *And the jigsaw puzzle is missing half a dozen pieces.* On a whim, she didn't turn in at the cottage but drove past the manor, following "the road to nowhere." *Which is exactly where I feel like I'm going.*

She imagined a hush as soon as she entered the woods. Close-growing trees arched over the road, darkening it with shadows. But they also created a setting that made her wish the Jaxon who'd dreamed of building a fairy-tale cottage in these woods had followed through. With no need to worry about holding up traffic, she drove slowly, looking left and right, to see if there were any signs left of that dream. A little more than a mile along, she reached the road's end without finding a clearing or any vestige of one. *Just a dead end in the woods,* she thought, and immediately wished she hadn't.

Faith called Eileen over a hasty lunch. "Sorry about the peanut butter sandwich in your ear."

"You should have stopped here while you were in town, and we could have had lunch together," Eileen said. "It wouldn't have been any less rushed, though."

"No, and this was just a trip to get the ants out of my pants. But I'm not sure it did much good." She told Eileen about meeting Corrie at the antiques shop and giving up on the stacks of magazines. "I did learn that other people have been asking about Michael Patrick material, including one of our guests."

"Is that so unusual?" Eileen asked.

"Probably not. I show off his books on tours of the library often enough. I guess I should be happy to know that anyone listens."

"If Corrie knew what's at stake, she might tell us who'd been interested in Patrick."

"Maybe. The other thing I learned might be more promising." Faith told about her stop at the bike shop and the news that Lindsey's husband no longer worked there. "There's some question about whether he quit or was given no choice. I texted Brooke. She knows they have money problems and car trouble, but said she definitely heard *works* at the bike shop, not *worked*."

"Lindsey might not have said anything about the job for any number of reasons," Eileen said. "But money problems could be a good motive for kidnapping."

"It doesn't strike me as the most logical solution. And a major step up from taking money from a till."

"You're right," Eileen said. "Kidnapping is hardly the go-to crime for a young couple down on their luck. If you need money for groceries, you don't ask for a priceless necklace and a rare book."

"But—" Faith said and stopped.

"But what?"

"What if you need an accomplice or two? One who has access to a specific building and another who has plenty of spare time to keep an eye on your intended victim? You might be able to persuade that unfortunate young couple to join you."

"Yes, you might. What's Lindsey's last name?" Eileen asked.

"Hannah. Dillon and Lindsey Hannah."

"I don't think they're regular library users, but I won't hold that against them. And money problems can happen to anyone—they aren't a reflection on anyone's character, so I won't hold that against them, either. But I'll see what I can find out about these two."

Brooke stopped by the Castleton Manor library that afternoon bearing a tray with a teapot and a plate of shortbread.

"How did you know I needed that?" Faith asked.

"I'm an angel in an apron." Brooke put the tray down on a table. "Plus I'm on break, so I brought two cups." She looked around. "It's quiet in here. Nice. Maybe the scrumptious lunch made them all take naps before the movie sucks them in."

Faith closed her laptop and stretched. "Sorry I can't give you an update in exchange for tea and cookies. No news from Midge, and the bike shop report was all I had. Nothing from Charlotte."

"No worries," Brooke said. "Well, that's not true. There are plenty of worries, but I know you'll let us know if you hear anything." She poured a cup and held it out to Faith. "You need this. Come sit down."

"Aunt Eileen talked to Charlotte this morning," Faith said. "She says the kidnapper's playing with Charlotte and maybe he's playing with us too. I think she might be right."

"Do we *know* the kidnapper's a man?" Brooke asked.

"No, but I'm tired of saying 'the kidnapper.' This is beginning to feel personal and I don't like this guy hiding behind anonymity. I want to know his name."

"Then we'll give him one," Brooke said. "I name him . . . Griff. I dated a guy named Griff. We went out exactly twice, and believe me, a creepier loser has never been dated by womankind on the face of this earth. That was the last time I ignored Bling and Diva's opinions about men."

"Griff. I like it," Faith said. "We'll tell Midge and Aunt Eileen. It's better if we avoid using the k-word, anyway."

"So we have a name for him," Brooke said. "But here's what else we don't know about him. We don't know what he's trying to accomplish. Why is he collecting things that he can't sell without getting caught?"

"Maybe they can be sold to someone with a very private collection," Faith said. "I've heard of ultrawealthy collectors who commission art thieves for specific paintings. But again, this seems more personal. I keep going back to the question of how he got Gloria out of her suite. What if she went willingly? Not because she's involved or because she was lured with Sir Arfer, but because she knows Griff? And whether she knows him or not, if she went with him willingly, she saw him."

"Or an accomplice," Brooke said. "Griff might stay in the shadows. That's just the way a low-down guy like that would operate."

"Aunt Eileen and I are thinking the same thing." Faith told Brooke about Lindsey and her husband.

"Desperation isn't pretty," Brooke said.

"I know you like her," Faith said.

"I do." Brooke let her hands drop in her lap. "Because she's sweet. But that's why she might've been able to get Gloria to go with her. If Gloria went willingly but is now being held against her will, she should be able to identify someone—an accomplice or Griff himself—when she's let go. And then we call the cops."

Faith slowly shook her head.

Brooke stared at her, then shook her own head. "Brother. Of course not. If she can identify anyone, then no one's letting her go." She closed her eyes. "This just gets worse and worse."

Faith shoved her empty teacup across the table. "Charlotte told Aunt Eileen she's going to the movie this afternoon. I have to catch her before it starts."

14

Lights in the salon hadn't dimmed for the showing of *Murder With a Splash of Larceny* yet, and Faith scanned the audience for Charlotte. Alyssa saw her and patted the empty seat beside her. Faith waved her regrets. She didn't see Charlotte. Tanya wasn't there either, but Jed sat in the back row. His head was bent, as so many others were, staring at a phone. *Should I?*

She walked to the back of the room and glanced down the last row toward Jed, still wearing his standard outfit, hiking boots and all. Of course, that didn't mean he didn't own running shoes. She walked along behind the last row, slowly, stopping every few feet. She hoped that if Jed was aware of her at all, he assumed she was stopping to look for someone, which she was. But she was also establishing a pattern of movement so that when she stopped behind him, it wouldn't be anything remarkable. When she did, she took a chance and positioned herself so she could see over his shoulder and get a look at the phone cradled in his hand.

Jed was looking at the weather report. *And what did I expect to see? Incriminating evidence? Get a grip.* Faith went back to the door. Still no Charlotte.

She decided to wait outside the salon in case Charlotte was running late. *If she's coming at all. It would make more sense to just call her and tell her I need to speak to her.* She stepped into the corridor and stopped short of bumping into Heath.

"Afternoon, Faith. Sorry, I didn't mean to make you jump."

Faith smiled. "It's not your fault. I'll blame it on too much tea."

"That sounds like the dilemma of a cozy mystery lover. They're prone to drinking tea, aren't they? Are you going to watch?" He nodded toward the door.

"Waiting for someone."

"Don't wait forever, Faith."

He tipped an imaginary hat and went in. Faith saw Alyssa wave to him and pat the empty seat again. When she looked back down the corridor, Charlotte was coming around the corner. And Charlotte must have seen her, because she turned right around and went back the way she'd come. Charlotte moved fast, but Faith was faster.

"Charlotte?" Faith kept her voice low and polite, but she moved in front of her and stopped, feeling like a sheepdog staring down a stubborn ewe. "Can we talk?"

Charlotte looked . . . haunted. Or hunted. Faith immediately felt like a bully for accosting her and reached a hand to the older woman's shoulder.

"The breakfast room is right here," Charlotte said, stepping back before Faith touched her. "It should be empty this time of day." She crossed the corridor. Faith followed. As soon as it was evident they were alone, Charlotte turned to her. "It's bad news, isn't it?"

"No! I'm so sorry if that's what you thought."

"Oh my," Charlotte said on a deep exhalation. "From the look on your face, I was so sure. Well, what *is* this about?"

"What we talked about Monday. The possibility that Gloria's being held here in the manor. I understand the danger of blundering around, but what if we talk to Wolfe and get his help? He knows the manor. He would be the best bet for searching quietly and carefully." Faith watched Charlotte thinking about it, her eyes cast toward the floor, a hand rubbing the back of her neck. "So much about this points to someone with intimate knowledge of this house," Faith pressed.

Charlotte looked back into Faith's face, her mind made up. "No."

It wasn't the answer Faith expected. "Charlotte, please."

"Wolfe cannot know about this. End of discussion." Charlotte started to move past her.

"Just one more question," Faith said, rushing her words to catch Charlotte before she left the room. "Do you have any idea, any suspicions at all about who's behind this?"

"I wouldn't want to know the person who could do this."

Faith stared after her, wondering if Charlotte believed that was a real answer. *Or is she hiding something?*

The showing of Gloria's film that afternoon was a hit among the attending mystery and suspense aficionados.

The only thing more exciting was the real-life drama of Lindsey catching Rachel Vail breaking into the du Maurier Suite. Faith was passing through the lobby when the call came in for the security guard. Hearing the du Maurier Suite mentioned, she followed him up the staircase.

"I was looking for evidence of a crime," Rachel insisted when the guard confronted her.

Faith was immediately on alert. Did Rachel know something about Gloria's disappearance? "You probably shouldn't say anything," she rushed to tell Rachel. She wanted to find out what Rachel knew, but now was not the time to spread the news of the kidnapping. And unfortunately, the commotion had attracted a number of other guests.

Rachel started to say something but stopped when Faith put a finger to her lips.

"Do you know this woman, Miss Newberry?" the guard asked.

"Miss Vail is one of our guests." Faith decided to take the initiative and suggest a course of action. "Would you like to question Miss Vail in Ms. Russell's presence? In her office?" Faith looked past the security guard to see Lindsey picking up Rachel's burglar "tools" from the floor in front of Gloria's suite. Lindsey—who'd happened to be in the right place at the right time to catch Rachel.

"Why don't I take Miss Vail and the tools down to Ms. Russell's office? I'm sure your expertise is needed here. You can meet us there after you speak to Lindsey. Rachel, will you come with me?"

"Believe me," Rachel said, "I look forward to being heard."

"I'll take responsibility," Faith said to the guard. With that, she took the tools from Lindsey, then took Rachel by the elbow and escorted her to the elevator. When the elevator door slid closed, she let go of Rachel's elbow. "Okay, tell me fast. What crime, what evidence, and what do you know about it?"

"She robbed me. I'm going to prove Gloria robbed me of the opportunity to get my work before a top New York agent."

"Is *that* all?" Faith hadn't meant to say that out loud and when she looked at Rachel's face, she was sorry she had. "I didn't really mean it like that," she said. But when the elevator door opened to the basement level, she felt as though she were backing out of a tiger's den. The tiger followed her out.

"You make it sound like it's nothing. It isn't nothing. It's *everything*. I did everything right. I enrolled in Gloria's expensive, exclusive online workshop. I wrote. I rewrote. And I rewrote again. To her specifications. She loved my premise. She loved my characters. She loved my setting. She loved my voice. She encouraged me to enter the prestigious First Chapters Contest. First prize was hand delivery, by her, of the winning entry to a top New York agent with an excellent chance of representation. *I* should've won that contest. She didn't judge it fairly and gave the prize to someone else. And chicken that she is, Gloria Bauer knows she's guilty. And do you want to know how I know she knows? Because she disappeared after she saw me at the reception Sunday night. That's the sign of a grade A, pedigreed, top-class chicken."

Faith had continued backing slowly down the hall toward Marlene's office followed by the nearly apoplectic Rachel. They reached Marlene's door, and Faith just had time to think she'd never been so happy to see Marlene when Alyssa erupted from the elevator and ran after them, followed by Jed.

"Where's Gloria? What does she know about her?" Alyssa shouted, pointing at Rachel. "What's she done with her? It's a cover-up. I knew it. Make her talk!"

"I've got this," Jed said. He spoke quietly to Alyssa. Faith didn't hear what he said, but Alyssa snapped her mouth shut on another shout of "Cover-up!" and walked back down the hall with him.

"What's going on with that woman?" Rachel asked, staring after Alyssa. "Is she all right in the head?"

Faith exchanged raised eyebrows with Marlene—another first.

"Please come in," Marlene said to them. "And close the door."

"Really," Rachel said, after she was seated in one of the visitors' chairs in front of Marlene's desk, "that woman has sounded like she has a screw loose all week. Nothing's happened to Gloria. She ran off when she saw me."

Seated and calm with an attentive audience, Rachel was happy to share her theory of Gloria's disappearance. In the spring, she told them, she'd splurged and taken an intensive online writing class from Gloria. Gloria proved to be an excellent teacher and a hard taskmaster. And she'd let her students in on the secret of finding their muse.

"The only muse you need is your bottom in the chair," Rachel explained. "That's what she told us. And I believed her. I still believe her. I wrote my heart out for that woman, and she said she loved my work. She went so far as to tell me she'd never had a student of my caliber in a workshop. What was I supposed to think? She ran her First Chapters Contest for the workshop registrants. She made sure I sent in my entry. I waited to hear that I'd won." Rachel took in and let out several deep breaths before continuing. "I didn't win. And I'm a big girl. I know there are no guarantees in life. But I wanted to talk to her face-to-face about it. Not online like we did in the workshop. Face-to-face. And that's how I know she threw the contest. She's guilty. She ran off because she knows she's guilty. And one way or another I'm going to prove it."

"Rachel says Gloria saw her at the reception, and that's when she left," Faith said.

"When she *ran*," Rachel corrected.

Faith saw dawning light in Marlene's eyes.

"But that's still no excuse for breaking into one of our rooms," Marlene said. "Why did you? The room's empty. It's been cleaned."

"All week I've been hearing that you expect her back. You've been spouting some cockamamie story that she's been called away—" Rachel stopped short. "I'm sorry. I didn't mean to suggest you're lying. But I thought she might have run off so fast that she left things behind and that's why you keep saying she's coming back. I'd love to find just one file, one note—"

"Don't even think about trying it again," Marlene said. The "tools" lay in a pile on her desk—two antique keys, a credit card, and a set of small screwdrivers. Marlene moved them around with a finger. "Would any of these even work?"

"Truthfully?" Rachel asked. "I have no idea. I didn't get any farther than putting my eye to the keyhole and trying to fit one of those old-fashioned keys in the lock. I bought them at the antiques shop in town. It was worth a try, but it turned out to be a waste of money."

Marlene hefted the keys in her hand. "They aren't too big or heavy. You could make a necklace, hang one in the middle. We have a craft room here, near the spa. You should do it. It could be real cute."

Faith chalked up another first for Marlene. She'd never heard her describe anything as "cute."

"Do you mean you aren't calling the police?" Rachel's eyes filled. "You aren't kicking me out?"

"I probably should," Marlene said. "But the guard texted me before you arrived. Lindsey says she only saw you kneeling by the door with your tools spread out on the carpet."

"Did you ask Lindsey how she happened to be so lucky to show up in the right place at the right time?" Faith directed the question at Marlene and tried to make it sound like relieved but idle curiosity. It was Rachel who answered.

"She got there right after I gave up on the key and was trying to figure out what to try next. When she asked if I was breaking in, I panicked. She scared the spit out of me, but I probably scared the spit out of her too. And really, I have to hand it to her. She kept her cool. She's a tough little thing, and I'd say *I'm* the lucky one. Lucky she showed up when she did, or who knows how far I would've gotten."

Rachel stood and offered her hand first to Marlene and then to Faith. "You're a peach, Marlene. Faith, you're another." Then she gathered her burglar kit. "Maybe I can get a refund at the hardware store for the screwdrivers. But a key on a necklace, huh? I like it." She handed one of the keys back to Marlene.

Faith walked with Rachel to the stairs. "I really am sorry about my 'Is that all?' comment. My mind was on a different track altogether."

"Hey, that was a minor mistake compared to the one I was making. But you know what? That mistake gives me an idea for a new book. Maybe even a series. And that means it's time to put the old muse back to work." Rachel ran up the stairs.

Faith was still standing where Rachel left her in the basement hallway when Jed came up and put his hand on her shoulder.

"You handle yourself well in a heated situation," he said. "Now I know who I'm sticking with if disaster strikes."

"Hi." Faith took a half step back to dislodge his hand. "Thanks for helping with Alyssa. How did you calm her down?"

"Bought her a lollipop in the gift shop." Jed grinned, then stopped. "That wasn't kind. I told her Rachel is just as worried about Gloria as she is. But Rachel shows it in a different and completely misguided way. That *is* right, isn't it? Or close? Say, can I buy *you* a lollipop?"

Faith laughed and started up the stairs beside Jed. "What you told her is close enough, and no lollipop, thank you."

"I think she might be slightly unbalanced," Jed said. "Both of them, if you want my purely amateur diagnosis. So can you tell me what's going on with Gloria? What's *really* going on? Because loose screw or not, Alyssa has a point. This isn't like Gloria. And if she doesn't come back, you've got to expect more guests to ask for partial refunds. Not that that would be a disaster for this place." Jed's gaze lowered as he climbed the stairs and pondered. "But people will be people, and they aren't happy when they don't get what they pay for. And word of mouth and online reviews? They go a long way these days."

Faith had stopped several steps below, her thoughts climbing another path. Could the kidnapper—Griff—be trying to ruin Castleton's business? Surely there were easier ways to do that. Unless Griff also had a sadistic streak and was having fun playing with Charlotte and watching her dance to his whims. Not to mention how he was using Gloria.

When Jed realized Faith had stopped, he turned back to her. "I'm sorry if I upset you. People tell me all the time that my internal editor needs an adjustment. Don't pay any attention to me. I'm sure none of that will happen. Especially if Gloria comes back. People love to forgive eccentrics." He spread his arms and grinned again. "They forgive me all the time." The grin disappeared on its own this time. "Folks want to know what's going on, though. An announcement with real information wouldn't be a bad idea."

"You're right. I'll mention it to Marlene. It will help if you mention it to her too. In the meantime, all I can say is that we really do hope Gloria will be back before the end of the week."

"Griff?" Eileen asked. She'd surprised Faith by meeting her in the manor library as Faith was getting ready to go home. Faith

had surprised Eileen with the name and the story of Rachel's attempted burglary. "And Marlene is satisfied with the story that Gloria left because of Rachel?"

"It ought to keep her out of our hair. Not that she's been in it. But if 'knowing' why Gloria disappeared eases some of her stress, then it's all good. A happy Marlene is a . . . a less unhappy Marlene."

"Griff," Eileen said again. "Well, as long as giving this person a man's name doesn't subconsciously keep us from considering he might be a woman. But whoever this creature is, Griff is a very nasty piece of work."

"Playing a vile game with us," Faith said. "Don't you get that feeling?"

Eileen cast uneasy glances around the library. "Do you ever feel completely alone here? I never thought I'd worry about you at Castleton Manor."

"None other than macho suspense writer Jed Knowlan says that I'm good in an emergency."

"That makes me feel better and more worried at the same time."

"Please don't worry, Aunt Eileen. But that reminds me. Can *you* convince Charlotte to let us search the manor?"

"I tried and failed this morning."

"That might be why she seemed especially cranky about it this afternoon. She must've felt like I was badgering her. I thought if we could talk to Wolfe about it she might go along, but she won't hear of it."

"Now would you like to hear my news?" Eileen asked.

"I jumped right in with mine and didn't even ask. Tell me."

"Brooke managed to get us invited for clam chowder with the guests this evening."

Faith flopped into an armchair.

"Exactly," Eileen said.

"Exactly what? I didn't say anything."

"You didn't need to. We're all feeling worn out."

"Is that how I look?" Faith sprawled farther. "There. Now even I recognize my lack of enthusiasm. Are you sure you don't want to join them, though? I'm sure I can whip up a tiny bit of energy, and it would be a good opportunity for suspect watching."

"What would we be watching for? I don't mean to sound so negative, sweetheart, but Griff, who might not even be here at the manor, is smart enough that he's not going to slip up at the dinner table over a bowl of clam chowder."

At the word "chowder," Watson roused from a nap on Faith's desk, ears alert.

"You're right." Faith closed her eyes and massaged her forehead.

"On the other hand, the clam chowder here is fabulous," Eileen said, "so Brooke is bringing enough for three to the cottage at six instead."

"Talk about saved by the bowl. Bless you, Aunt Eileen. Who am I entertaining?"

"Brooke and I will be there. Midge has supper plans with her husband, of all things."

"The nerve. Come on, Watson." Faith pulled herself to her feet. "Let's go home and rearrange the dust for our dinner guests."

15

In front of Faith's fire, over bowls of excellent, creamy New England clam chowder, the three members of the Candle House Book Club who were present agreed that it would be impossible to keep an eye on all their suspects.

"*A*," Brooke said, "with so many guests it would be obvious if we stuck like glue to just a few of them. But we'd have to do that or risk losing them in the crowd. And *B*, we aren't whittling the list of suspects down—we're adding to it."

"*C*," Eileen added, "we all have jobs. And some of those jobs aren't at the manor."

"What about you, Faith?" Brooke asked. "Do you have a *D* for us?"

"I want to go back to *C*," Faith said. "But not *C* for *careers* at Castleton Manor. *C* for *coincidence*."

"I don't believe in coincidences," Brooke said.

"I'm suspicious of them myself," Faith said. "On the other hand, the word exists for a reason, and sometimes coincidences exist as well. Here's what I have. One of the books I showed the guests during the library tour was a copy of Patrick's *Grimm's Fairy Tales*. One of the ransom demands was for the same. Rachel Vail asked about Michael Patrick material at The Fishwife's Attic. Rachel was caught trying to break into Gloria's suite—by Lindsey. Rachel claims she was looking for evidence to prove that Gloria rigged the results of a high-stakes writing contest she judged." Faith looked at her friends. "So how much of that is *C* for *coincidence* and how much of it is really *C* for *connection*?"

"You forgot about the interview with Tanya yesterday," Brooke said. "You gave her a choice between Prince Charming and Rumpelstiltskin. They're both characters in Grimm stories, right? For a second there, it looked like she wanted to spit some of her poison at you."

"That was my fault," Faith said. "She made a crack earlier. Something like she'd probably heard all my questions before. And she was interested in Patrick's Rumpelstiltskin, so I thought I'd try for a question she wouldn't see coming. I felt bad afterward."

"Don't worry about it," Brooke said. "She seemed fine later and it ended well, with a stampede for my cashew-pistachio bars on the refreshment table. Stampedes are a beautiful sight. But back to keeping track of our suspects—I thought of a way I can keep better tabs on Lindsey. She's mentioned a few times, in passing, how much she likes to cook and wishes she had more time to do it. She envies our huge kitchen, even if it is in the basement. So I asked her to work extra hours with me in the kitchen. Told her I'd show her a few tricks."

"Given our suspicions," Eileen said, "is that wise?"

"Have you ever seen me with a rolling pin or skillet in my hand?" Brooke asked. She mimed swinging a baseball bat.

"Please be serious, Brooke."

"I am always serious in my kitchen, Eileen. Besides, it's a moot point. Lindsey can't take the extra hours. She says her husband is away on business and she can't afford the extra daycare or a sitter."

"That's interesting," Faith said.

"On business?" Eileen asked. "Did he get a new job?"

"She didn't say it was new," Brooke said. "It could be. But it also made me wonder if she even knows he lost his bike shop job."

"Or if she even knows where he is?" Faith asked.

"That too."

"There's very little to find out about either of them in town," Eileen said. "She isn't local, and they've both kept a low profile. If she's on social media, she keeps her security buttoned down tightly."

"Did you get an address?" Faith asked.

"A tiny, tiny studio apartment on the way out of town on Falmouth Road," Eileen said. "I drove past it before coming here. Did I say *tiny*? With two small children and not enough room to swing a cat."

"Or a kidnap victim," Brooke said.

Eileen shook her head. "I don't know how she handles it."

The cat had learned to recognize the signs and symptoms of stress in humans when he and his own human lived in the city. The pinched eyes and pained forehead, crossed arms and drawn shoulders, knees bouncing or fingers tapping, the lack of attention to cats—specifically no one offering the cat a taste of chowder that smelled so beautifully of cream and something divinely fishy.

But this evening, the humans' sad inattention to a cat's immediate needs also had a plus side. The youngest of the three humans, the one who talked about fish as though they had intelligent thoughts in their heads, was sitting on a cushion on the floor in front of the fire. She waved her hands when she talked so that they looked like the branches of a tree on a windy day. She had put her bowl down, the better to flail her hands, and the cat took the opportunity to help his human by reducing her burden of housekeeping chores. He licked the bowl clean.

Faith got to her feet. "Your bowl's empty, Brooke. I'm going for seconds. Can I get some for you while I'm up?"

"Sure. In a clean bowl, please. I didn't empty this one, and I have a feeling I know who did." Brooke raised an eyebrow toward Watson, who vigorously washed his face.

"Aunt Eileen?"

Eileen shook her head. "At what point do we stop listening to Charlotte and go to the police anyway?"

"That's a really good question," Faith said, "and I've been giving it a lot of thought."

"And?"

"I still think we'll hear from Griff again. But if we don't—"

"By this time tomorrow," Eileen said firmly. "If we don't hear from him by this time tomorrow, we go to the police."

"Okay. Now, whatever else Jed might be, I've decided he is really good at sizing people up and knowing their strengths. I told you he said I'm good in an emergency, right? Here's the proof. We're going to forget seconds on the chowder, because it's for times like this that I keep an emergency stash of ice cream."

"Good thing I brought some of the cashew-pistachio bars too," Brooke said.

Faith and Watson curled together in front of the fire after

Eileen and Brooke left. Watson was thoughtful enough to lie beside her and let the laptop have her legs. He of course never changed out of his dapper tuxedo, but Faith had changed into her favorite old sweats and had knotted her hair back with a scarf. Then she'd cleaned out her backpack, purse, notebooks, pockets, and anyplace else she'd tucked the notes and scraps of paper she'd jotted thoughts on. Now they were spread out on the floor, waiting like so many pieces of the jigsaw puzzle she seemed to be putting together. A wind had risen, and Faith wondered how tight the cottage windows would be against the winter gales sure to come. Then she realized that the Jaxon family would have made sure that even the gardener's cottage was in peak condition.

"It sounds like November is finally blowing in, Watson, but we'll keep warm with our books and our fire." Faith rubbed Watson between his ears. "And each other."

While Watson purred, Faith traveled back through time by reading Gloria's daily posts to her blog. She'd dipped into the blog when she was preparing for Simmering Suspense Week, but her appreciation for Gloria's writing and wit grew the more she read. The posts were a mix of writing tips, recipes, book news, random musings, and an occasional guest post. Several of the guest posts were from Jed. There was a search function in the blog's sidebar, but Gloria wasn't good about tagging her posts so they could be searched. Faith tried *class*, *contest*, *judge*, and *judging* with no luck. When she tried *workshop*, she found what she was looking for.

"Rachel was telling the truth about that, Watson. About the existence of the online class, anyway." Faith found a brief mention of limited registration for a workshop. Unfortunately, she didn't find a roster of attendees or any posts about a First Chapters Contest.

But that made some sense. Rachel had said the workshop was exclusive and not heavily advertised because Gloria had wanted to make the experience more valuable. Faith didn't find any blog posts during the weeks of the workshop or after that talked about entering contests or judging them.

"Oh. Watson, look at this."

She had found an allusion to contest horror stories, not in a post, but in a comment Gloria had left on one of Jed's guest posts.

"It's right here, Watson. He talked about problems he'd encountered in judging blind submissions to anthologies and contests, and in a comment she said, 'Been there, been accused of that. Hope I don't live to regret it.' It isn't proof of anything, but it sure raises some questions."

She opened a file on the laptop and pounded out her frustration with questions by typing out the new ones. *Is Rachel the victim here? Or is she Griff? But if she's Griff, then why was she breaking into the suite? In broad daylight, for crying out loud? Or is she the world's best actress and she did all that to throw us off the scent?*

Faith was breathing hard by the time she finished pounding the keys. She stroked Watson's head until she felt calmer, then saved the document and closed the laptop. "Do you ever get tired of questions, Rumpy? Don't answer that."

A knock came on the front door.

"But maybe we'd better answer that." First, though, she set the laptop on the chair and went to peek around the edge of the curtain. Wolfe Jaxon was at the door. Her notes and scraps were still spread across the floor. *Not good.* "Hang on!" she called to the door. She madly scooped up papers, put them in a pile on the end table, grabbed a book, and placed it not quite squarely on the pile. Then she opened the door.

"Hi. I know it's kind of late," Wolfe said. "I hope I'm not interrupting anything."

"Not at all. I'm always happy to see you. Come in."

A gust of wind came in with him. Faith shivered and closed the door harder than she meant to while Wolfe walked over to greet Watson. *The sign of a nice man,* she thought, watching as they touched noses. *Nice man wearing a very nice sweater.* She looked down at her sweats and laughed.

Wolfe looked up. "What?"

"Nothing. I was just thinking how beautiful your Aran is and how right for the change in weather. Then I realized you caught me in my unstylish loungewear."

"Which probably means I *am* interrupting something. I know how precious a quiet evening can be."

"It's fine. Really." She went to the fire and poked the logs to stir it up a bit. "Can I get you anything? Tea? Cocoa?"

"Can I take a raincheck on that?"

"Of course. Care to sit down?" She took the laptop from her chair and tipped her head toward the chair's twin.

"Sure."

But rather than sit, Wolfe picked up the poker and stirred the fire as though Faith hadn't just done that. It wasn't like him to hem and haw, but something was up, and the possibilities of what that something might be worried her.

The cat lost interest in the human conversation when the male turned down the offer of cocoa. Not that the cat wouldn't have turned

down cocoa, but a taste of the milk that went into it would have been another story. However, he'd heard a tantalizing rustling and skittering noise when the male human brought the swirling wind into the room, and that might be worth his time to investigate. He slipped to the floor, silent and sure, cunning and courageous, and slunk behind and past the humans.

Wolfe nodded at the laptop in Faith's hands. "See? You were busy. And I'm kind of—I don't have much time, and there are a couple of things."

Faith couldn't decide how to make him more comfortable. When he stayed with his back to the fire, she put the laptop back on her chair. He'd sunk his hands into his pockets, but she could see the impression of his knuckles through the corduroy, which made her think he was clenching his fists. She leaned her elbow on the back of her chair, hoping she looked more at ease than he did.

"I noticed something," he said. But he stopped there and rocked back on his heels, looking at the floor as though he might want to argue with it. Then he looked up, looked at her. The hands came out of his pockets and he gave them a shake. "I'm worried about my mother. Have you noticed anything odd with her?"

"I don't really know your mother very well," Faith said. Carefully, truthfully. "What have you noticed? What are you worried about?"

"Specifically, there's a book gone from the locked cabinet in the library, and I'm virtually positive she removed it. Not that that's a problem. That's not the point."

"Why do you think she has it? What is the point?"

"I saw her with it," Wolfe said.

"You can't get much more positive than that."

"But she says she never had it. And I've never known her to lie like that."

"Maybe she forgot?" Faith said. "What's the book?" *Please don't say—*

"Patrick's *Grimm's Fairy Tales.*"

At the corner of the end table the cat froze. There, blending in perfectly with his surroundings, he sniffed the air, separating the comfortable scents of his human and the sharper scents of the male from the smells the wind had brought in—dead leaves, watchful mice, cowering beetles, and the prickly smell of cold itself. He was disappointed that no actual mice or beetles had run through the door with the wind. A few leaves had blown in, but the cat dismissed them. Leaves could be entertaining, but he'd found the source of the enticing rustle and skitter. Some of his human's scraps of paper had blown off the table onto the floor. Moments ago, before his human opened the door, the cat had seen her hurrying to remove these papers from sight. And so, always ready to lend a paw, the cat followed his human's excellent example and set about batting the papers under the table where no one would see them.

"If she forgot, that worries me," Wolfe said. He started to pace in front of the fire. "But that's where the problem comes in, because I don't think she did forget. I think she really is lying. I'm also virtually positive she knows that I know she's lying."

"I can see why that would be disturbing. When and where did you see her with it?"

"She had it in her suite Tuesday morning. And again, having it isn't the problem. She has as much right to any of those books as I do. But later, I wanted to show the book to someone. I asked her about it, and that's when it became a problem."

And it means she didn't take it straight to Aunt Eileen for the pickup box. Why not? And she never did say what she was doing between finding that second note under her door and bringing it here. Faith wanted to pace too, but there wasn't room for both of them. "Huh."

"What?" Wolfe asked. "You just said 'huh,' as if you'd thought of something."

"Just a question. How do you think I can help?"

"It's a private library, but you do keep records. I'd just like to know, did she borrow the book?"

"Ah." Faith didn't like what she was going to say next. "This is going to sound incredibly priggish, but librarians don't tell. Even in private libraries."

"Which is as good as telling me that she did."

"No, really, it isn't. Partly because—" She spread her arms to take in the room and spotted Watson. *What's he up to? Oh dear.* She refocused on Wolfe and spoke quickly. "Partly because I don't have the records here, so my answer wasn't based on having them in front of me and knowing yes or no. But if I did have them here, that would still be my answer, whether your mother took the book or not. Just a second."

The book she'd put on top of her notes hadn't done the trick.

Some of them must have blown off onto the floor. Watson held one down with his paw and looked up at her.

"Sorry," Wolfe said. "They must've blown off when I came in. Here, let me."

"No, that's okay. I've got them." Faith scrambled to sweep the notes into a pile before he could get to them. She got to her feet, holding the notes to her chest. *Like a demented squirrel gathering nuts I don't intend to share.*

The cat was congratulating himself on his good deed when his human swooped in to finish the job. He stepped aside. Her dedication to teamwork was a facet of her personality he admired. Now would be a good time to show just how much he admired it by applying yet another layer of fur to her ankles, although now that he noticed, that might prove difficult. The small amount of space between his human and the male seemed to be growing smaller. It was good, then, that he had a maneuver or two up his sleeve to fix such problems. He hopped onto the end table, positioned himself for optimal trajectory, and pushed the book and the rest of the papers off.

Wolfe looked from the mess to Faith. "Well," he said finally, "I'd better be off, then." Without another word, he strode to the door and out into the cold night.

Faith looked from her armful of papers to Watson. "Wolfe wasn't happy about that, Watson. And I can't blame him, but I couldn't let him help pick up the mess you made." She clucked her tongue. She wasn't happy either. Her notes hadn't been in any kind of order to begin with, but now they were definitely worse. And on top of that, when Wolfe had arrived, he'd said he had a couple of things on his mind, but he'd left before telling her what the second one was. And it wouldn't help to ask Watson what had suddenly gotten into him that made him need to dump her stuff. He would just blink and act innocent. She sighed and shook her head. "You . . . sweet old hooligan in a tuxedo."

The cat sat on the expanse of bare end table. His human sometimes looked at situations from the wrong point of view. Point of view was important for finding out about and surviving in the world. That was why he performed experiments. By watching some things fall, by turning others over, and by wrestling others around a room, he gained the satisfaction of seeing them from multiple perspectives. Now, hearing the unhappiness in his human's voice, and seeking to impart some of his own satisfaction from this approach, the cat blinked. His was a good human, but she was wrong about so many things.

16

Thursday morning, Midge called Faith to report on her efforts to identify likely places a kidnap victim could be held. "It was a wild goose chase," she said. "I know it was."

"No luck?"

"Worse. I got reported for suspicious behavior. Officer Tobin stopped me and asked if I'd seen *another* light blue Subaru Forester driving slowly and snooping around closed summer cottages. As if I didn't know he was talking about me and my vehicle. He was being nice."

"Giving you a chance to fess up? Oh, Midge, I'm sorry."

"That's okay. He didn't have any problem with me. He even gave me a cover story. He's the one who came out when Peter called about Sir Arfer the other morning."

"So Mick thinks you're looking for Sir Arfer?"

"Which is kind of what I am doing," Midge said. "Mick asked why I was cruising in that area in particular, and I told him the truth. That I knew it was a long shot, but I felt terrible and needed to do something. He said be careful and wished me luck. So I'm going to keep looking and it's all good."

"Unless Griff saw you snooping."

"I'd say that's unlikely. But that's also why we pay you the big bucks in this detective outfit—so you'll do all the worrying."

Faith laughed. "Funny, I don't recall getting a paycheck."

"Consider the next bag I bring from Snickerdoodles your first one. Talk to you later."

Faith disconnected and stared out the window. She *was* worried.

What if they'd made a huge blunder by not calling the police at the beginning? They hadn't heard anything from the kidnapper the day before. Nothing overnight. Unless Charlotte had heard something but was no longer telling them. *At this point, would it be a bad thing if I call the police myself? Can they do anything this late?*

A woman who might have been Miss Marple come to life was knitting in front of the great fireplace in the library when Faith arrived. Faith recognized her as one of the guests who'd thought Alyssa's antics were staged and part of the week's entertainment. The woman finished a round and waved the free needle. Faith called good morning, saw the blank look on the woman's face, then noticed her earbuds. The woman waved the needle again, fussed around in the chair until she found her phone, and gave it a poke.

"What I call reading," she said, pulling out one of the earbuds. "I'm listening to Agatha Christie's *The Body in the Library* and wanted the right atmosphere. My hands like to stay busy, but my mind loves disappearing into a book. This is my compromise."

"Nice. What are you knitting?"

"A Christmas stocking for my sixth grandchild. But I dropped my ball of red wool and someone kit-napped it."

Faith stared at the woman. For a split second she thought the woman knew about Gloria.

"Kit-napped. I was making a joke. A cat pounced on it and carried it out the door."

"Oh dear." Faith couldn't help a smile of relief. "Black and white? Stumpy tail? Heart full of larceny?"

"It was the stumpy-tail end of that ball too. It's still attached, though, so it doesn't matter. I can just keep going and the yarn will keep coming from wherever he carried it off to. And at least he didn't get my full ball." The woman held up a ball of red yarn the size of a large apple. "He looked so proud of himself and silly at the same time. I didn't have the heart to take it away from him."

"You're kind to be so forgiving. I'll see if I can get it back."

"Books, knitting, cats," the woman said. "They're all I need in life."

"Hey!" A gray-haired man leaned around the side of a chair, startling Faith. "Don't let her kid you," he said. "Back rubs from her husband are pretty darn good too."

Faith left the two of them chuckling together and went to find the Great Tuxedoed Yarn Hunter and his prey, following the strand that led from the woman's stocking. She spotted Watson farther down the gallery. *Just like a small boy, playing ball games in the house.* She shook her head and went after him.

"Watson," Faith called.

Watson dribbled the yarn ball, feinting left and then right.

"Watson."

Calling to him did no good, so she stopped pretending it would. Running to catch him wouldn't help either. He'd just go faster. So she followed behind, admiring his fancy footwork and waiting for him to lose interest or for the chance to catch him off-guard with her own footwork. Her patience paid off when he swatted the ball and made a goal behind the refreshment table set up for the morning's program. She stooped to get the ball, but Watson playfully swatted it under the table skirt and then sat back as if to say, "Ta-da." Faith sank to her haunches, then lifted the skirt and crawled under to reach the ball. Watson came along for this lark, rubbing his head on her elbow. She wiggled her eyebrows at him and pounced on the ball before he could.

Then Faith heard a voice.

"I told you." Low and tight, the voice was on the other side of the table. The tip of a shoe poked under the table skirt, white like the shoes Brooke wore in the kitchen. Faith held her breath. Watson sniffed at a stain on the shoe's toe. "No, I told you. It'll be paid. *Re*-paid. Whatever. You'll get it."

Faith wasn't sure, but she thought the voice might be Lindsey's. She didn't sound like the sweet young woman Brooke talked about, though. And she didn't sound tearful or worried as someone might who was at the end of her rope or resources. This voice was hard and in control. Faith hoped whoever it belonged to didn't lift the table skirt. She looked at Watson. *What have you gotten me into now?*

"Poison," Tanya said to the rapt audience in the gallery later that morning. "It's an attention grabber, isn't it? Poison can be lethal. It can be elusive. And interestingly enough, it can be just what the doctor ordered, because medicine taken incorrectly or by the wrong person is poison. Here's something else I like to remind people who take my Pleasantry of Poison workshops." Tanya came out from behind the podium on the low stage. "Give a man a fish, and he eats for a day. Give a man a poisoned fish, and he eats for a lifetime. Think about it."

Faith listened to the groans from the back of the audience with relief. Gloria had been scheduled to present her popular Perils of

Poisons program this morning. When Tanya had offered to fill in with a version of the workshop she presented at writers' conferences, Marlene accepted, but with some trepidation. Gloria had become something of a poison expert over the years and her "routine," as Gloria had called it, had been eagerly anticipated. The guests seemed just as happy to be listening to Tanya, though. Faith heard equal numbers of laughs and gasps at Tanya's recommendations for lethal doses of easily obtained poisons.

After yesterday's interview, Faith had had her own reservations about the program, but things seemed to be going well enough. The chairs were full. Alyssa and Rachel sat together in the front row and Jed sat several rows behind. *Good. Some suspects together where I can easily watch them.* They weren't doing anything at the moment except listening to another suspect tell them how to kill people. *Great.* She looked around. *Where's Charlotte and how much do I need to worry about her absence?*

"Foxglove, oleander, daffodil," Tanya said. "All three are beautiful and, when used properly, or improperly, deadly. They're all grown right here at Castleton Manor. I checked with the gardener to verify that. Isn't that nice? But don't worry. I'm almost positive—almost—that none of them have been used in this morning's treats." She gestured toward the table at the side of the room under which Faith and Watson had so recently hunkered. A startled Lindsey, setting out trays of refreshments on the table, looked back at the audience now avidly watching her and gave an uneasy wave.

Tanya reclaimed her audience with a reference to mushrooms, and Faith sidled closer to Lindsey and tried to get a look at the toes of her shoes. It wasn't going to be easy. Lindsey was busy and moving around the table. When she did stand still long enough, her toes were under the table skirt. Faith decided against crawling under the table again. But when Lindsey finished and stood back from the table for a final check, Faith moved next to her.

"Looks delicious," Faith whispered.

Lindsey answered with eye contact and a gratified smile.

"Brooke says you like to cook."

Lindsey broke eye contact and Faith quickly looked down.

"You should go for it," Faith whispered. She patted Lindsey on the shoulder and moved back around behind the audience, her mind muddling through her "shoe evidence." She chided herself for not being clever enough to have thought of whipping out her phone while she was under the table and taking a picture of the stained shoe. Now she knew that Lindsey's shoe had two stains on the toe, but she wasn't sure how many she'd seen under the table. She wondered briefly if Watson would be able to recognize the shoe in a sniff test, then dismissed the whole idea as ridiculous and grasping at straws.

Marlene appeared in one of the gallery's arched entries, scanning the audience. She circled the perimeter and came to stand beside Faith.

"How's it going?" Marlene asked quietly.

"Really well. She's not as charismatic as Gloria, but she's a good speaker. I don't know much about poisons, but she sounds like she knows what she's talking about."

"Bottom line—are the guests happy?"

Just then the guests laughed at something Tanya said. Marlene looked pleased.

"She has good timing," Faith said.

"As long as no one who's laughing now complains later." Marlene held up a brown package the size of a paperback.

Faith felt a cold whisper of dread brush the back of her neck. She was aware of Tanya's voice, of Marlene's eyes, of the package. She didn't want to ask what it was, but she didn't have to.

"A mysterious package arrived for you," Marlene said.

Faith didn't automatically reach for it. She noted a few heads turned toward them and felt uncomfortably conspicuous.

"I looked for you in the library," Marlene said, "because that is where you should be. And you *shouldn't* be receiving personal mail here at the manor. Please don't let it happen again."

Marlene shoved the package at Faith. Faith took it and left the gallery to go to the library.

She made a tour of the room to make sure she was alone. Only Watson was present and napping in his favorite chair. She touched his warm head in passing and then sat down at her desk. She bounced back up again immediately, too nervous to sit.

Her name was written on the package in the same looping letters used to address the envelopes to Charlotte. Only her first name. No address or return address. Brown paper taped around a box.

She set the package on the desk and took a pair of cotton gloves from a drawer. Pulled them on. Took a breath from deep inside. Slit the brown paper wrapping with a letter opener.

Inside was another of the lavender envelopes and a white gift box. She stared at them both, her hands folded in front of her to keep them from shaking. Then, suddenly infuriated, she slit the envelope, yanked the note out, and read it.

I told Charlotte not to tell anyone. She told you and your friends. Now things are not going so well for Gloria. They will get even worse if you don't do exactly as I tell you. Get me $500,000. Persuade Wolfe. That should be easy for you. Tell him to get it by midnight tonight. When he has it, tape a piece of white paper in your front window. Then wait for the next instruction. Now do you *believe that I'm watching? I will know if you contact the police. At the first sign of police involvement, this is over, and not the way you want it to be. DO NOT play games, or this is the last you'll see of Gloria Bauer.*

Faith lifted the lid of the white gift box with one hand, her other hand clamped over her mouth. Coiled inside the white box was a long gray braid of hair. Gloria's hair.

17

Faith didn't touch the coil of hair. She dropped everything onto the surface of her desk, then covered it all with a section of the weekly *Lighthouse Bay Chronicle*. She peeled off her gloves and backed up, panting.

A half-million dollars. Ask Wolfe for a half-million dollars. And Gloria's braid is buried on my desk. She threw the newspaper aside, exposing the awful pile on her desk again, afraid she was going to be sick. She placed the lid back on the box. Watson came and rubbed around her ankles. She picked him up, held him close, and walked to the middle of the room. The kidnapper was sure she could talk Wolfe into handing half a million dollars to her. She wasn't sure she could talk him into having lunch with her after the way she'd acted last night. After the way she'd been acting anytime lately. She buried her face in Watson's fur.

"Faith?"

Feeling her heart do a flip-flop, Faith looked over Watson's head at Charlotte. She paused half-in, half-out of a door that had opened in the walnut paneling near the fireplace. Wolfe had previously shown Faith that door, but it was so perfectly fitted into the panels that it was undetectable until the second it silently opened. Heath Westcott was behind Charlotte.

"Always a pleasure, Faith," Heath said. He smiled at her over Charlotte's head.

"You startled me," Charlotte said. "I thought everyone would be in the gallery listening to the poison lecture." She stepped into the library, followed by Heath, letting the secret door close behind them. Faith had never seen the ordinarily meticulous owner of Castleton Manor wearing jeans, a flannel shirt, and a bandanna over her hair. The shirt was a man's and hung to her knees. "Why *aren't* you in the gallery?" Charlotte demanded.

Faith didn't know how to answer a question that came across as both accusatory and ridiculous without sounding defensive. Nor did she know how to answer it in front of Heath. He was also in jeans, a departure from his usual trousers or suit. She forced her mouth to move. "I was. Marlene told me I should be here."

"Never mind," Charlotte said. "I was going to come find you at some point anyway."

"Charlotte's just given me a complete tour behind the scenes, as it were, for old times' sake," Heath said. "I hate to say it, Charlotte, but Blake's tours were more exciting. If you want to meet his standards, you need to turn off the lights and run away. Now, if you don't mind, I think I'll go catch the rest of Tanya's poison recipes. Thanks for letting me tag along."

Charlotte pulled off the bandanna and used it to brush at a cobweb on her shoulder. Watson wriggled in Faith's arms. She let him down, and he went to crouch in front of the concealed door, dipping his head to sniff at the place where Charlotte and Heath had appeared.

"I was going to let you know," Charlotte said, "what I found. Or didn't. And I don't know if it's good or bad. But it seemed the best way."

Faith stayed quiet, waiting to find out what Charlotte was talking about, letting the other woman's words fill the space between them. She hardly dared think of Gloria's braid and the demand for money sitting on her desk and what it might mean if Charlotte had told Heath about the kidnapping.

"Well, he told you where we've been." Charlotte flung her arm toward the door, making the bandanna in her hand flutter. Making Watson jump and slink away. "You've been so anxious to have the 'secret rooms and passages' searched. Now I can tell you that there's no sign Gloria has ever been anywhere in them. And they aren't really secret."

"'Hidden,' I think I called them," Faith said, breaking her silence. "Rarely used, anyway, and not open to the public. Why on earth did you search them with someone who had no idea what might be involved? Unless you told him."

"No."

Faith knew she was crossing a line. She could picture the fit Marlene would have if she heard the way Faith was speaking to Charlotte, but there was so much more at stake than her job. She had to make Charlotte see that. And Charlotte so obviously knew more than she was telling. "Why would you put someone at risk like that, much less yourself?"

"For two perfectly good reasons. I didn't expect to find anything, so I expected it to be safe, and . . ." Charlotte hesitated, then sounded almost pleading. "I needed to do *something*."

"I can understand needing to do something." *And I can believe it*, Faith thought. *So why don't I believe her first reason?*

"So that's that," Charlotte said. "I don't know what else to do at this point except keep waiting."

"We can call the police."

"No."

"Charlotte, come here and look at this."

Faith had Charlotte put on the cotton gloves before she let her read the new note. And she told her what was in the gift box so that it wouldn't give her the same shock she'd had. Charlotte shook her head and said she didn't need to see, couldn't bear to see. She'd gone pale. Faith made her sit down and pulled a chair around so they faced each other.

"Charlotte, at this point, it isn't just your call anymore. This package had *my* name on it. The kidnapper has been watching all of us. The threat is escalating." Charlotte didn't respond, and Faith couldn't tell if she was getting through to her. "We're gambling with Gloria's life. We have no guarantee she'll be freed even if we turn over the money. This person might ask for even more. He or she might even take someone else and hurt more people."

"I should have asked him to stay." Charlotte's lip trembled.

"Asked who to stay, Charlotte?" Faith kept her voice calm, hoping her frustration didn't show.

"Wolfe left for London this morning."

Faith's thumbs flew as she sent a group text to the book club members. She did her best to report the package and its contents in as few plain and dispassionate words as possible. Her fingers stumbled several times in the effort. She summarized the note. She couldn't make her fingers type all the wretched words.

Brooke responded first: *Horrible! Are you in library? Be right up.*

Stay put. We're being watched, Faith wrote back immediately. Then her phone rang, and she dropped it. "Aunt Eileen. Sorry—"

"No, dear, I'm sorry. I can't do this in texts. I need to hear your voice. I need that much contact to know you're all right. Brooke is absolutely right. This is horrible. Have you spoken to Charlotte? She must be beside herself."

"Hang on, Aunt Eileen. Let me tell Brooke and Midge that I'll catch them up later."

"You can do that without hanging up?"

"You need to get a smarter phone. They're very convenient. Just a sec." Faith lowered the phone and tapped out a quick text, then raised the phone back to her ear. "There. Done. Unless autocorrect kicked in and I just told them I'd cram the spout later or something ridiculous." She giggled.

"If you're laughing, does that mean there's some good news somewhere?"

"No. That's just your garden-variety hysteria bubbling up."

"What did the new note say exactly?"

"Is the gist enough for now? I locked it all in a drawer, and I don't want to look at it again." While Faith talked, she left the library through the French doors and stood on the terrace. "Aunt Eileen, there's more. I'm outside now, so no one can hear me. I want you to just listen for now, okay? I need you to hear what I'm saying and then tell me what you think."

"I'm ready."

"It starts with last night. Wolfe came to see me after you and Brooke left." Faith told Eileen about Wolfe's worries and questions and how they only added to her own.

"She—" Eileen started to say.

"Not yet. There's more. She searched the hidden passageways."

"That's a good thing."

"Maybe not." Faith told her about Charlotte taking Heath Westcott with her into the passages. "She said she didn't tell him why, and he seemed to think it was for old times' sake. She said she was sure it was safe because she didn't expect to find anything. But remember, she wouldn't let us search. And when I asked her to let Wolfe look, she refused. They didn't find anything and, as she said, that might be good or bad. But her answer to that problem isn't to finally call the police. It's to keep waiting."

"And then you told her about the package and the new note?"

"And she told me that Wolfe is suddenly out of the country."

"What did she say about getting the money?"

"She said she'd be in touch. Aunt Eileen, Charlotte's hiding something. I know she is."

"I'd like to defend her," Eileen said. "Or explain. But I can't."

"I have to go," Faith said. "I see guests in the library and I'm freezing out here. I'll be back in touch."

"Soon." It was more a command than a question.

"Soon." Shivering, Faith went back inside to see if the guests wanted help with anything. And to find out what Lindsey was doing there.

The knitter who'd lost her ball of yarn to Watson's soccer game that morning greeted Faith with a wave of her friendly needles. "Did you get a chance to hear any of Tanya's lecture?"

"Some of it. I enjoyed what I heard," Faith said. She peered around the woman. Lindsey was at the other end of the room and seemed to be looking under chairs.

"I enjoyed it so much that it made me paranoid. I made my husband take a bite of my scone before I did. That's why he isn't here now."

"That's ni—*what*?"

The woman laughed. "A joke. You go on. You've got work.

Miss Marple and I have a date with our knitting." She sat down in the chair near the fire again.

Lindsey's search was taking her closer to Faith's desk, and Faith went to intercept her. "Can I help you?" she asked. "Is something lost?"

"Someone reported a teacup." Lindsey straightened and looked at Faith. "She said there was a 'stray' teacup under a chair." Lindsey stifled a giggle with the back of her hand. "Like it ran in here on its own. She should've asked me to *fetch* it." She giggled some more, then composed herself. "Sorry. It made me think of *Beauty and the Beast.*"

"That's my husband's bad habit," the knitter called. "The cup's here, under this chair. Honestly, *men.* I apologize."

Faith waited while Lindsey got the teacup, then walked with her to the door. "Thank you for following up on that. That kind of careful attention is one of the reasons the manor is so beautiful." *Am I laying it on too thick?* Lindsey looked wary, but Faith had thought of something. She looked back and saw that the knitter had her earbuds in. "I didn't get a chance to thank you for reporting the attempted break-in yesterday."

"Oh. You're welcome." Lindsey looked distinctly uncomfortable.

"It's lucky you were right there." Faith paused while Lindsey stared into the teacup. "Did anyone ask you how you *did* happen to be there?"

Lindsey looked up. "No. That kind of surprised me."

"Was it luck?"

"I've never had luck. Not good luck, anyway. It was like the letter for Mrs. Jaxon that somebody told me to pick up in the du Maurier Suite. And this teacup thing. Someone stopped me and told me."

"That someone was trying to break in?"

"That something weird was going on up there."

"Any idea who that was?"

"I don't know her name. She's been around all week. She might be the one who jumped up and yelled something at you on the stage Monday morning. I didn't see her face then, but it might've been her."

Watson sauntered in at that point. She watched him walk right on past the stain on Lindsey's shoe without even a casual sniff.

"Did you need anything else?" Lindsey asked.

"No. Thanks, Lindsey."

Faith followed Watson over to her desk. He leaped up onto it. She sat down and got out her laptop. "Time to make a decision, old man. To call or not to call, that is the question." She fired up the machine and opened the file she'd pounded questions into the night before. "More questions," she whispered to Watson. There was something about whispers he seemed to like. He stretched his head toward her and she kissed his ears. "For luck," she said.

Then she opened a new document on the computer and listed all the knowns and unknowns she and the book club had come across, thought of, puzzled out, or stumbled upon in the past few days. Two columns—one not long enough, the other giving her the willies. She looked over at the knitter. Keeping calm and knitting on. "Keep calm," she whispered to Watson. "I want to do one more thing."

She went to Captain Angus Jaxon's map case in the far corner of the room. She would have liked to meet the man who sailed the seas, then came home to build this amazing house. He'd apparently loved books as much as she did and, she thought, probably shared the same feeling for maps. The large, flat drawers of the case contained his collection of antique, obscure, and downright fanciful maps. She enjoyed imagining a young Wolfe Jaxon sliding out one of these drawers on a stormy day and deciding which town or country or ocean to explore. The map Faith wanted was in the drawer labeled Local Area and State. Watson and the knitter came to see what she was spreading out on one of the library tables.

"I love detailed area maps," the knitter said. "This one's quite good, isn't it? The town, the manor, the lighthouses." She traced a finger along a side road. "Property lines, even. My husband is completely sold on his online mapping websites, but I still like the picture I get in my head from looking at a physical map. Maybe it's something to do with this kind of expanse. The spatial aspects of a large paper map as opposed to something on a screen. I wouldn't be surprised if paper and screen use different parts of the brain. What are we searching for?"

The area they were looking at—Lighthouse Bay and the several miles surrounding it—was huge. It was too much, too many properties and possibilities. Not all of them suitable for keeping a kidnap victim and her dog, but still too much.

"A needle in a haystack," Faith said. "With not quite enough information."

"You'll get there eventually," the knitter said, patting her hand. "Librarians usually do. I'm qualified to say that. I retired after thirty-five years with the UMass libraries, most recently in Lowell. I'd do it all again in a heartbeat. I'd rather have your job, though. Beautiful cat, beautiful books. And knitting." She rubbed Watson under his chin. "If you know which side your paw is buttered on, young man, you'll take good care of your human."

The cat looked at his paw and was only mildly disappointed to find that it had no butter on any side. Butter was all well and delicious in its place—on his human's toast or ear of corn, for instance—but a buttered paw required much cleaning. A clean paw was a stealthy paw. He stretched his paw out now and patted the large rectangle and small rectangles that represented the manor and the cottage. Then he patted a spot he'd recently explored.

Faith called Eileen, but only to tell her to expect a text. "And to let you hear my voice, but I want Brooke and Midge in on this—"

"Without being overheard," Eileen said. "Understood. Over and out."

Faith composed the text carefully using complete sentences. She wanted no misunderstandings. She explained the file they would find attached with her lists of knowns and unknowns, which included her concern that Charlotte was hiding something. She admitted feeling defeated. At the end of the text she wrote, *We can discuss what we know and what we don't know forever and still get nowhere. I want to call the police. What do you say?*

Eileen answered first, then Brooke, then Midge.

Call the police.
Call them
Call
I'll call Jan Rooney and let you know what she says, Faith wrote.
Brooke sent back, *All for one and one for all.*
Nice thought, Faith wrote, *but no. Explanation in a sec.* She took her time composing again, so she could convincingly explain why she should talk to the police on her own—so they wouldn't all be in hot water if there were repercussions for not going to the police at the very beginning.
Jan will understand, Eileen replied. *I'm sure it will be fine.*
Faith wished she could be as sure.

The cat knew the overwhelming burden of being faced with a difficult decision, such as choosing between two tasty morsels. He knew the sting of regret when the morsel not taken then scurried away, never to be pounced on again. He watched as his human, her face reflecting the burden of her own decision, coiled the cord for her laptop and tucked them away in her backpack. He had contemplated—and tasted—a variety of cords during his lifetime. Cords sometimes led to interesting places, much like paths in the woods and through marshy areas where he had to shake water off his feet every so often. Sometimes those paths led to places where he could learn . . . interesting things.

18

Officer Jan Rooney of the Lighthouse Bay Police Department was predictably annoyed after listening to Faith's report of a kidnapping at Castleton Manor.

"I know this whole thing is awful," Faith said at the end of her rehearsed speech, "but believe me, what we're most concerned about is Gloria's safety."

Faith and Watson had gone home, and she'd made her call from the safety of the cottage. She knew the kidnapper was watching the outside of her residence, but at least she could ensure that no one else was inside it, unlike at the manor with its hidden rooms and passages. She'd breathed a sigh of relief when she asked for and was put through to Jan Rooney. She liked and admired all the local officers, but Jan was especially popular in Lighthouse Bay. Jan stuck to the rules, but she also offered a shoulder when one was needed, and Faith was pretty sure she would need one by the time she finished telling her story.

She'd practiced what she would say so she wouldn't slip up and involve the rest of the book club. She did include Charlotte, telling herself that she had to include her, not that she was doing it because she felt Charlotte deserved whatever soup she ended up in. Faith gave Jan Rooney credit for listening to her entire recitation without interrupting.

"You're most concerned for the victim's safety," Jan said, "but you didn't call the police."

"No. But that's because we really *are* worried about her. The letters implied she'd be killed if we told you."

"That 'we' is you and Charlotte Jaxon? Was she following your lead?"

"I thought it made sense to offer her my help," Faith said.

"I'm noting in my report that you didn't really answer my question. Also that you waited *four days* before calling us. But I also understand that threats like the ones in those letters aren't easy to handle."

That might have been a throwaway line for Officer Rooney, an all-purpose phrase from a handbook on the psychology of dealing with the interfering public, but Faith doubted it. "The other thing I'm worried about," Faith said, "is the book. By no means does it come before Gloria, but it's old and somewhat fragile."

"What's it worth?" Officer Rooney asked.

What are they worth? Faith could hear someone else asking that when she'd given the tour of the library on Monday. But who had asked?

"Miss Newberry? Faith?" Officer Rooney's patience lasted only so long. "How valuable is the book? And what about this necklace?"

"No idea whatsoever about the necklace. And I don't know an exact amount for the book. It's part of a set though, so it's not quite as valuable on its own. And depending on who has it now, it might be more valuable in pieces." The image of Gloria's gray braid coiled in the box flashed through her head. "Someone might slice out the illustrations and sell them individually. Jan, I know it's just a book, but that would break my heart. But even that's nothing compared to Gloria. I'm so sorry."

"Is Marlene Russell aware of the situation?"

"Only that Gloria's gone, but she believes Gloria was upset about something and left."

"And the room was cleaned," Officer Rooney said.

"It was obvious she'd been there when I went to check on her Monday morning—bed slept in, towels used, but nothing of hers left at all."

"And *then* the room was cleaned?"

"Except . . ."

"Except what, Faith?"

"Backing up to Monday. The bathroom smelled of lavender. The manor provides almond- and vanilla-scented toiletries. The ransom notes and envelopes are lavender colored too, which made us think they were her own paper. And then, yes, the suite was cleaned. There was no hint of the lavender the second time I went in."

"The library hold locker, where you delivered the necklace and book—how did you arrange that?"

"By requesting the box and code the kidnapper asked for," Faith said. "Charlotte put the necklace in on Monday and the book on Tuesday."

"I've used those boxes. They're handy. But when I use them, the codes only work once. So, for instance, if you opened the box to put the necklace in, how did the kidnapper use the same code to get the necklace out?" Officer Rooney, back to being patient, waited for Faith's answer.

Faith pictured Jan Rooney like a very large Watson waiting to pounce. "Um . . ."

"So you've had the help of a few friends. We might talk about that more later, but here's something I'd like you to think about. I've read a fair amount on the psychology of criminal behavior—"

"Jan, we really didn't mean to do anything wrong!"

"I'm glad to hear that. I'm not talking about you and your 'we,' though. I'm wondering about the box number and the access code. Were they random choices, or were they chosen for the kinds of reasons people choose lottery numbers? Even criminals follow patterns."

"Both times it was box three and the code was 1004."

"Ten-four," Jan said. "That's part of the ten code some police departments use. Ten-four means message received and understood."

"Could that have anything to do with this?" Faith asked. "I wonder if one of our suspects is an ex-police officer?"

"*You* do not have suspects, Faith. And now, you will turn every piece of evidence that you have over to me."

"But you can't come out here to get it, and I can't go to the station," Faith said in a rush. "The kidnapper is here at the manor, watching. But listen. I know what we can do. You give me, say, an hour, and then go to Happy Tails, the pet food bakery. That'll give me time to get there and back here so there's no chance of anyone seeing us together. Everything will be waiting for you at Happy Tails in one of their bags."

"What makes you think you can trust the clerk at Happy Tails not to look in the bag?"

"Sarah is Midge's most trusted employee. But if it'll make you feel the evidence is more secure, I'll wrap it in a box like a birthday present and put that in the bag. Sarah would never open someone else's birthday present."

"Don't be ridiculous."

"Jan, *please*. This will work." Faith waited and finally heard a heavy, very controlled sigh.

"Fine. And any notes you've made, they go in the doggy bag too. Because although I don't think I know you as well as I should by now, Faith, I somehow doubt you and your 'we' have been sitting and twiddling your collective thumbs while all this has been going on. For the *past four days*."

"Everything. I promise. Give me an hour and it'll all be there."

Faith hadn't promised that she wouldn't make copies of her notes and the ransom notes. She scanned them all and printed off her document with the lists of knowns and unknowns. She put the originals of her notes, the print of her document, the ransom notes, and the box with Gloria's sad braid into a slightly larger box. Feeling half-silly and half like a secret spy, she wrapped that box in paper dotted with balloons and tied it with ribbon. Then she put the "gift" into the Happy Tails bag she'd brought home on Monday with the Tunaroons and Shrimp Whiskers. She tucked the bag inside her backpack, drove into Lighthouse Bay, and left it with Sarah, telling her it was a surprise for Jan Rooney. She made it back home fifteen minutes before the hour she'd asked for was up. And in case the kidnapper was watching her or the cottage, she made the reason for her trip obvious by swinging a small Happy Tails bag in her hand. The bag contained a sample of something new for Watson.

"I think the trip into town did me some good," she told Watson when she was home again. Her head felt clearer. Or maybe it was the phone call to the officer that had reamed out the cobwebs. That woman was long-suffering, but she was a good friend and a better policewoman. They weren't out of the woods with this, but she felt a little better about their chances. And Gloria's.

Watson stared at the Happy Tails bag in her hand.

"Would you like to know what Sarah sent? She's calling them Savory Salmon Meowdeleines, but she wants your opinion before she sells them to the general public. You've become her go-to consulting expert."

Watson led the way to the kitchen and Faith tipped a few of the shell-shaped tidbits into his bowl. He immediately started "consulting." She made herself a quick sandwich and leaned against the counter while she ate it.

"You know, I have to give you credit too, Rumpy. Something about you plopping down on the map and patting around on it this morning must have registered in my subconscious."

On her way back from town it had clicked into focus. The kidnapper might be the one who'd reported Midge to the police when she was driving around. If Midge was getting too close to where he had Gloria and Sir Arfer, then he might have gotten worried and complained to the police as a way to get rid of her. If Midge could tell them where she'd been before Mick Tobin stopped her, maybe they could help the police narrow down the search.

The cat was mildly affronted by the suggestion that his carefully considered and adroit actions with the map were no more than "plopping" and "patting around." They should have provided conclusive evidence of his systematic and scientific information-gathering prowess. He was, however, only mildly affronted. Humans, even his own, had difficulty seeing the whiskers for the fleas, or as they more prosaically put it, the forest for the trees. He was satisfied with his human and glad that he'd given her a good idea. And surprisingly, hearing the loathed "Rumpy" had given him an idea.

After her hurried lunch, Faith headed back to the manor. She had her interview with Jed to prepare for—and dread. Watson walked across the lawn with her, dashing left and right every so often to pounce on leaves.

Faith enjoyed his antics and reflected on how often watching him and his joyful approach to life put things into perspective. When he saw something that needed to be pounced on, he pounced. She decided to take a lesson from him and treat the upcoming interview the same way. It was there, it needed to be done, and she would do it. She filled her lungs with chilly November air and then let it out.

They'd reached the terrace and Watson climbed the stairs with her, but then he stopped and sat on the top one.

"Not coming in? It's chilly, sweetie." She looked at the sky. Scuds of clouds sailed fast and high in the clear autumn blue.

Watson came and rubbed around her ankles, but when she moved toward the door he turned and trotted to the stairs at the other end of the terrace.

"Be careful out there, Watson," she called after him and then, more softly, "I love you, old boy," as she watched him disappear down the steps.

Faith looked at the sky again. It might be blue, but it felt heavy and gray.

When she opened the door, Alyssa blew toward her like a thundercloud.

19

Faith, her eyes on Alyssa, waited until she was almost upon her, then slipped sideways out of Alyssa's path. Alyssa's clutching hand missed grabbing Faith's arm by inches. Alyssa stumbled slightly and put the clutching hand to her chest.

Faith circled Alyssa, not sure what to expect, ready to run. Alyssa pivoted inside the circle, her eyes on Faith. When Alyssa moved the hand from her chest to her mouth and hiccupped with a sob, Faith stopped.

"What's going on, Alyssa?" Faith asked sharply, then immediately felt terrible for venting her exasperation. "I'm sorry. You, of anyone here, know what a stressful week this has been."

"I do know," Alyssa whispered. Faith realized with a start that the woman was crying. "And that's why I can't believe this." They were alone in the entry but she looked over each shoulder in turn, cringing, before she continued. "Tanya and I were supposed to eat lunch together. She promised. I'm the president of her new fan club and I'm going to organize Team Tanya online, to help her market her books. We were going to talk strategies over lunch."

"What about Gloria?" Faith asked. "I thought you were *her* number-one fan."

"I have a big heart," Alyssa said. "And Tanya made me see that Gloria really must have 'flaked out,' as she put it."

"Okay. So you and Tanya were eating lunch together."

"We were *going* to eat lunch together. But I walked her to her room this morning and I haven't seen her since."

Faith wanted to say, "So what?" but couldn't, not with everything else that was going on. Dread sank into her belly. "You knocked on her door and called her phone?"

Alyssa nodded. "And texted."

"Maybe she decided to meet you there, or . . . forgot and went somewhere else."

Alyssa shook her head. "I waited outside her room."

"For how long?"

"Half an hour."

"You were there the whole time?" Faith asked.

"Close enough."

"I'm not sure close enough counts. She might have come out and gone anywhere."

"It was close enough to spit," Alyssa said. "Now, I don't usually lose my temper and say rude things like that, but I've discovered that I have a nose for trouble. And right now my nose is twitching, and I want to know what you're going to do about it." Alyssa put her hand to her mouth again, her eyes brimming. "I am so sorry. But you seem to know how to handle situations, and I'm worried sick."

Faith patted her arm. "I am too. Hang in there. I'll get reinforcements and we'll see what's going on."

"I'm quite frankly surprised you allowed me to come with you," Marlene said as she and Faith stepped off the elevator on the second floor.

You aren't the only one, Faith thought. Aloud, she said, "Alyssa's excitable."

"No arguments there."

"But from what she said, I think there really might be cause for alarm."

"Well," Marlene said, "if there's one thing I'm good at—"

"Shh, this is Tanya's room," Faith said, glad for an excuse not to hear any more about what Marlene was good at.

They knocked but heard nothing.

"It's possible she went somewhere," Faith said.

"But you don't think so," Marlene said, studying Faith's face.

"And I'd feel better if you, as manager—"

"Take the lead?" Marlene raised a finger, dipped into a pocket, and produced a key. "The master. Stand back. I'll go in first."

Marlene might be prickly, but she was fearless. But even Marlene had to gasp at the scene that unfolded inside the room. Faith looked around her and sucked in her breath.

Tanya lay curled on her bed, motionless, eyes staring. A soda bottle sat on the bedside table. A glass and a small amount of spilled brownish liquid lay on the bed near her hand.

"We need to call the police and the ambulance," Faith said.

"I will."

That was fine with Faith. There were papers spread out on Tanya's desk. She stepped over and scanned them. "Hey!" Marlene hissed, making her jump. "Don't touch anything!"

"Right. I won't."

Marlene put her phone to her ear and turned her back.

Faith took out her own phone and snapped pictures of the papers, reading what she could in a hurry. They appeared to be notes about Jed Knowlan's career. One or two had underlined portions. One passage that mentioned Gloria had a large exclamation mark in the margin next to it. Faith got a close-up. The exclamation mark had been made with such zeal it was almost engraved in

the paper. She really wanted to shift the papers enough to see—
Marlene was finishing her 911 call. Faith slipped her phone
into her pocket.

Based on what they called "evidence found at the scene,
preliminary interviews, and information received," Officers Rooney
and Tobin cautioned Marlene and Faith not to talk about the
details of the scene. They took Jed back to the police station with
them. Faith tried unsuccessfully to find out what information
they'd received and whether Jed was under arrest.

"Thank you for your concern," Officer Rooney said to her. "We
appreciate your civic involvement, but we will take it from here."

Faith rubbed her face and watched them go. She and Marlene
broke the news of Tanya's death to Alyssa. Alyssa collapsed in
Rachel's arms, and Rachel accompanied her to her room, promising
to stay with her. Marlene said she would tell Charlotte and make
announcements to the rest of the staff and to the guests. Faith
retreated to the library. She sent a text to the book club, then
scrolled through the photos on her phone, quickly closing the
screen when Charlotte appeared.

"My dear," Charlotte said, taking both of Faith's hands in
hers. "Come over here and sit with me."

Faith went with her to the chairs by the French doors. When
they were both seated, Faith blurted, "I told the police about Gloria."

Charlotte leaned her head against the back of the chair and
closed her eyes. "I am so relieved."

"*What?*" Faith sat up straighter.

Charlotte's eyes came open. "That sounded incredibly callous and I didn't mean it that way. Tanya's death is a dreadful tragedy. But my relief, my profound relief, comes in knowing that all of this stops with Jed Knowlan's arrest."

"So he *was* arrested?"

Charlotte nodded. "I'm so tired, Faith. I can't tell you how tired. But I want you to know how grateful I am for everything you and your club members tried to do. It's been such a nightmare." She'd closed her eyes again, or she might have seen the dumbfounded look Faith knew was on her own face.

"Are you saying Jed kidnapped Gloria? Has she been found?"

"All this time I've been so afraid. Because of everything we thought we knew about the kidnapper, I worried that my son Blake was involved. As a scheme to get more money from his brother."

Suddenly, Charlotte's actions over the last few days made some sense. Not that Faith could totally excuse her. "And the necklace? And the book? He couldn't have fenced them."

Charlotte shook her head. "I didn't know. It didn't make sense, but Blake always has some scheme. He's always felt a tremendous rivalry with Wolfe, his eldest, responsible brother. If I'd told Wolfe, he would have been furious. I was frightened and angry myself. And ashamed. But now I'm relieved. I'm sure Jed will tell them where Gloria is and the police will free her."

"Has Blake been around lately?" Faith knew of Wolfe's youngest brother, but she'd never met Blake and wasn't sure she'd recognize him.

"That's part of what worried me. He hasn't been, and I thought he must be in hiding. I'm sure I haven't helped the situation, but he is my baby and I've tried to do what I can to keep my family together."

"Have you tried calling Blake?"

"Calling him would prove nothing," Charlotte said. "With cell phones, he could answer and be anywhere in the world."

"That's true." *And that's another reason Tanya's death doesn't clear him. He could still be anywhere, possibly somewhere close to home.* There was no connection she knew of between Jed and Blake, but it still seemed that someone with an intimate knowledge of the manor and Lighthouse Bay was involved. So if Jed was the kidnapper, maybe Blake was the accomplice they'd been wondering about.

Charlotte pushed herself from her chair. "I'll let you get back to work. I'm going upstairs for a long nap."

After Charlotte left, Faith pulled her phone out again and studied more carefully the photos she'd taken of the papers on Tanya's desk. They seemed to be evidence of an obsession with Jed's writing and his career, but could they be evidence of kidnapping or murder? Faith didn't see it, but something gnawed at her about them. The way they were laid out on the desk, so obviously making Tanya look suspicious of Jed—had Tanya laid them out like that? She might have, of course. But if Jed killed her—why? Because she was digging into his past? Then why wouldn't he have destroyed the papers?

Faith decided to go home early. She wasn't feeling frightened so much as cautious, and crossing the lawn to the cottage before the sun went down seemed like a wise idea. As she was getting ready to leave, she saw Heath and Marlene talking in the main lobby. She stopped to thank Marlene.

"There's no need to thank me. I was doing what I'm paid to do—hold this place together." Marlene looked almost insufferably proud of herself, but then she softened and thanked Faith for her part.

"You're welcome, Marlene."

"It did occur to me that *you* might have had something to do with her death."

Faith felt herself gaping.

"Because of your insistence that we go up together," Marlene explained. "But I've always had a suspicious streak. Anyway, I was glad when they arrested Jed Knowlan so I could stop wondering about you."

"Oh. Well thank you for that too." *I guess.*

"I don't see it being Jed," Heath said. "The whole thing is unreal. But Jed? It seems to me that poison takes someone with more finesse. That's not exactly Jed, is it? Would he even know what kind of soda Tanya drinks? Frankly, I think Jed would kill Alyssa before he'd kill Tanya. And I'll stop there, because that was inappropriate, and I apologize. Are you leaving, Faith? Would you like me to walk you home?"

"Thank you, but no. I'll be fine."

She walked back to the cottage deep in thought. Something was wrong with the way their puzzle was turning out. Faith knew she was missing some crucial pieces. She didn't like to doubt the police, but she was very much afraid Officers Rooney and Tobin were fitting their pieces together the wrong way. She had a hunch that meant it wasn't over yet.

When she reached the cottage, her hunch was confirmed. Someone had tried to shove a lavender envelope under her door.

Faith grabbed the note, its one edge crumpled. She whirled around but saw no one, heard nothing. She fumbled her key into the door, pushed through, and slammed it shut when she was inside. She tore the envelope open with a finger, then couldn't read the blurred words because her hands shook. She dropped the note on the end table and bent to read it there.

> *My accomplice served her purpose and Jed is serving his. Wolfe might have flown the coop, but the money is still due. The time is still midnight. When you have it, tape the paper in the window. Think of it as your white flag. Tanya was expendable. So is Gloria. No police.*

Faith ignored the last instruction. She immediately called Officer Rooney.

"Did anyone get *in* the house?" Jan asked.

"No no. Even the note didn't get in. But it proves Jed isn't guilty."

"It doesn't prove anything, Faith. When we picked him up, he was walking across the lawn. Said he'd been running. He could easily have left the note to make us think he's in the clear. He writes this stuff for a living, remember? Speaking of which, how can someone who kills as many people as he does in his books be so squeamish about it in real life? He's been pale and shaking since we arrested him. I almost feel sorry for him. The one thing he does know how to do is clam up. He isn't talking. I'll come out and get that note."

"Jan? If you come get it, I won't be able to sleep. Because if I'm right, then the real kidnapper is still here and will see you and know that I called you. But if you're right and Jed left the note on my door, then you can wait until tomorrow to get it because you've already got him."

"Faith, I'm not dropping by Happy Tails again, or anyplace else."

"I'll bring it first thing in the morning."

After hanging up, Faith called the people she should have called first—the book club. She asked them to bring over their laptops and be prepared to stay. "We need to figure this out and finish it tonight."

"What if Griff is watching?" Eileen asked.

"I'm sure he is, and that's why I didn't want Jan coming out. But he already knows we're working together. And I get the feeling he's pretty confident we can't solve this. I say let him watch us."

Eileen, Midge, and Brooke arrived individually. Each time Faith went to the door to let one of them in, she called for Watson, but he didn't come. Not that he always did. Or even often did. But by now she was ready to worry about anything, and it didn't seem right to have a book club meeting—even one like this—without him.

"How's the mood at the manor?" Midge asked Brooke. "How are the guests taking these latest developments?"

"It's dismal. It couldn't really be anything but, considering. And dinner tonight was supposed to be based on Jed's book *Choked*."

"That doesn't sound appetizing at the best of times," Eileen said.

"We couldn't let the food go to waste," Brooke said, "but we reprinted the menu cards and left off the quotes and any mention of the book. And Marlene is dragging out her beloved party games to 'cheer everyone up,' as she says."

Midge groaned.

"I hear you," Brooke said. "But maybe they need that kind of fluff tonight."

"I just thought of a favor I need to ask Marlene," Faith said. "Hold on." She called Marlene and asked if she would call during dinner and tell her who wasn't there.

"Our authors won't be."

"Besides the obvious, Marlene. Please, it's important."

"So important you can't walk back here and see for yourself?"

So much for our moment of solidarity. "Don't worry about it, then, Marlene. Mrs. Jaxon can probably do it."

"I didn't say I wouldn't. I'll call you later."

"Thanks." Faith disconnected. She looked at her three friends, waiting in various chairs with laptops ready. "Shall we start with questions?"

"You just did," Brooke said with a wicked grin.

Faith rubbed her hands. "Good. Here are some more. Think of this like one of Marlene's party games, except we won't have a timer or a buzzer. Ready? Why kidnap Gloria?"

"Because she's worth money," Eileen said. "But except for her necklace, he didn't ask for her money."

"That we know of," Midge said.

"True. But the half million is Jaxon money," Eileen said. "Here's my question. Why ask for the *Grimm's Fairy Tales*? It's beautiful and it's valuable, but it isn't *ransom* valuable."

"Griff has a thing about *Grimm's*," Brooke said. "I think it's a—I'd say obsession, but maybe passion is more polite."

"I don't know if we need to be polite about him," Eileen said. "What about the Patrick connection? You go on with your questions. I'm going to look up Patrick again."

"Here's what I wonder," Midge said. "We don't think Jed is Griff, right? So what if Tanya wasn't really involved in the kidnapping either? This latest note said she was expendable, but does that prove she was involved?"

"Sir Arfer kind of freaked out at her, remember?" Brooke piped up. "When she tried to take him from me after he landed in the strudel. Maybe he recognized her."

"But if she was the accomplice," Midge said, "why kill her?"

Faith pointed at the note on the end table. "He said she'd served her purpose. Plus, now he wouldn't have to share the money with her."

"But what *was* her purpose?" Midge asked. "What if she was killed to throw us off? She might be a red herring. *Oh my gosh.* I just thought of something."

Eileen's fingers froze. Faith and Brooke sat forward.

"Sorry," Midge said. "A lightbulb moment for Happy Tails, not the case. I suddenly realized I need to come up with a recipe and start selling Red Herrings for cats. Sorry, I'll just go get a glass of water and calm down."

When Midge came back to the sitting room, Faith told them why Charlotte had acted as though she were hiding something.

"Because she was," Brooke said. "Bless her heart."

"Except she thinks Blake is in the clear now, which he really isn't," Faith said. The four women turned to their laptops, each pursuing a search related to the case. Faith focused on studying Tanya's website. She didn't remember a Grimm or Patrick connection from when she prepared for the week's programs, and she still didn't see any. She saw no obvious connection to Jed or Gloria either, but Tanya's digs at Gloria throughout the week seemed more significant now.

And what about that awful book signing? Faith went to Tanya's event calendar and found a list of recent bookstore appearances. She recognized some of the stores in the Boston area and knew they weren't remainder outlets. But Tanya had said the store had an appropriate name, and from the website, Faith could see that during the summer Tanya had signed at one called The Brick Book End—definitely an appropriate name for the place she'd described. The name was half-familiar to Faith, but she didn't know why.

Midge, meanwhile, paused in her typing and slid a map from her computer satchel. At Faith's questioning look, she said, "I'm pulling up a real estate website and cross-checking empty rentals and houses for sale against the roads I drove down."

Marlene eventually called and let Faith know they'd had a full house for dinner.

"Thanks, Marlene."

"Thanks to the games. They loved them. We only had one minor squabble, and that was during the *Sound of Music* trivia contest. Two players each claimed their birthday was closest to October 1—that date being appropriate because it's Julie Andrews's birthday."

"Nice. Thanks for the update, Marlene."

"My birthday too."

"Even nicer. Happy belated." Faith might have just barely heard Marlene still talking when she disconnected.

Brooke, hunched over her laptop, looked slightly guilty.

"What?" Faith asked her.

"Pool of suspects down by two. I should've thought of this before. I always look my dates up on this site before agreeing to go out with someone." She looked up at the others. "County inmate search. Dillon Hannah has been in jail for the past month. *That's* the business trip Lindsey told me about. And Faith, that car that ran you off the road? I think it was Lindsey. I heard her telling one of the other maids that the mechanic she took it to says the brakes and steering are shot on her car, and she worried she was going to run off the road earlier this week. Apparently this mechanic is hounding her for payment to fix the car, and she's having some trouble coming up with the money. She was so terrified by the car and her lack of money that I'm not sure she even saw you on the bike."

That explains the phone call while I was under the table. "And I guess even if she had, she couldn't have stopped to see if I was all right."

"We need to try to do something for that family," Eileen said. "And speaking of doing something, on a different note entirely, here's a celebration our two libraries should plan together. It'll be Michael Patrick's 150th birthday next year on October 4."

Faith froze. "His *birthday.*" Her heart pounded hard. "Ten four!" Without explaining herself, Faith called Marlene. "Marlene. Which two guests squabbled over having birthdays close to Julie's and yours?"

"That pushy woman who thinks she's the only author left at the manor."

"Rachel Vail?"

"Yes."

"Who else, Marlene?"

"Heath Westcott."

"What are their birthdays?"

"I can't be expected to remember that kind of trivia."

Faith forced herself not to growl with frustration. "Where are they? Heath and Rachel. I need to know."

"I have no idea. For heaven's sake. I'm at home."

Faith disconnected again and looked at three spellbound faces. "The code," she said. "The after-hours pickup box access code. It isn't a random number. It's a date—Michael Patrick's birthday, and I bet you anything it's also Griff's birthday. I think we're down to two suspects. Rachel Vail and Heath Westcott. But what do we do now?"

"Let your cat in for starters," Midge said. "I hear him at the door. But wait—Faith, *wait*."

Faith stopped with her hand on the doorknob.

"Make sure it's *him* and make sure he's *alone* before you open the door."

Brooke was already at the window, hands cupped to see better. "Yep, it's him."

Faith, her heart beating again, opened the door. Watson strolled to the center of the sitting room, and then, as though he'd arrived just to entertain their guests, he launched into what Faith called his crazy cat dance—leaping straight up, twisting, pouncing, and repeating.

"Silly Rumpy," Faith said. "I'm glad you got home in time for our meeting. We've made a breakthrough."

He stopped and looked at her, which surprised her because he usually turned away or stalked off when she called him Rumpy. But now he sat and aimed several tentative licks at his flank.

"What happened to your tuxedo, Watson?" Faith asked him.

"Pine sap and pine needles, et cetera," Midge said, getting down on her knees next to him. "You've been out exploring where you probably shouldn't have been, haven't you, Mr. Debonair? And you'll make yourself sick cleaning it off. Faith, I need olive oil and paper towels. Come here, sweetie." She pulled him into her lap. "Auntie Midge will clean you up."

Watson seemed perfectly happy to let Midge massage olive oil into his fur and paw pads. She itemized the oddities as she removed them.

"Twigs. Bits of gravel. Nasty honeysuckle. Where did you pick that up? We should find out and get rid of it."

When Midge was done with his cleaning, Watson strolled over to greet Eileen and Brooke, and then he sat down next to the map Midge had left on the floor. Faith picked it up and thanked him for not sitting on it.

Map. I haven't asked Midge the map question. "Midge, where were you when Mick Tobin stopped you?" She looked over at Watson. He blinked his slow cat blink of approval. "Anyplace within cat distance of Castleton Manor? Maybe someplace with pine and Japanese honeysuckle?"

"Cat distance, as you call it, can vary," Midge said. "A lot. They've done some very cool studies using GPS tracking devices attached to collars that show—"

"Approximate, Midge," Eileen said. "I think Faith is onto something here." She took the map from Faith. "For instance, what's this line you've drawn here?"

"My best guess at small dog distance." Midge sat down between Eileen and Brooke.

Faith left them to it and watched as Watson walked over to the end table and sniffed at the narrow space between it and the floor. Then he poked the space with an exploratory paw. When he lay down on his side and worked at getting something out from underneath, Faith went to get her ruler.

"What have you found, Watson? Are you a clever boy or a naughty one?" She swiped the ruler in from the side, catching whatever he'd found and pushing it out. Some of her notes on scraps of paper. And a business card.

"Got you, Griff," Faith said triumphantly as she read what was written on the card. "Watson, you're a rascal and a genius. We are down to one," she said, turning to the others and holding up the card. "Ladies and fellow Candle House Book Club members, Griff the kidnapper is Heath Westcott. He's a bookseller at The

Brick Book End. Tanya did a signing there over the summer. That's his connection to her. He spent a few summers here as a kid and knew Blake Jaxon. That's his Lighthouse Bay connection. Michael Patrick's birthday is October 4. I think Heath's is too. That's his Patrick connection. The *Grimm's* connection comes through Patrick and Tanya. Tanya was interested in the Patrick edition of *Grimm's*. She asked to borrow it."

"The Brick Book End is more of a bargain basement than a bookstore," Eileen said. "It sounds snooty, I know, but I stopped in there once and it even smelled like a basement. It would be a depressing place to work for anyone who loves books."

"Maybe he wants to get out of it," Brooke said.

"Tanya wanted to quit her day job and just write," said Faith. "Kidnapping is an extreme way to go to finance a dream."

"Anyone else want a soda while I'm in the kitchen?" Brooke asked, getting up.

"That's it," Faith said. "*Soda*. That's the connection proving Heath and Tanya were in this together and he killed her. But poor Marlene, I have to call her again."

Faith made the call, apologized, and asked one last question. "Did you tell Heath Westcott that the poison that killed Tanya was in a bottle of soda?"

"*A*, we don't know what killed Tanya. *B*, the police asked us not to divulge any details of the scene. So no, I did not. If you can avoid it, please don't call me again this evening."

Faith thanked Marlene, apologized again, and disconnected. "When they hauled Jed away, Heath said poison took finesse and Jed wouldn't even know what kind of soda Tanya drank. No one told Heath there was poison in the soda. He knew because he put it there."

"Excellent," Midge said. "Now we know who. But we still need to know where Gloria is. We're getting closer. Our dog distance and cat distance arcs intersect and give us a smaller area. Can we find out where Heath stayed when he was a kid? It seems like it would have to be kid distance from here."

"Hold on," Faith said. "Heath knows where she is and we know where Heath is. If we want to find her, let's catch him."

"How?" Brooke asked.

"Simple. He told us how."

21

"*Simple* is a dangerous word," Officer Rooney said when Faith called and told her their plan. "*Simple* is a lot like 'Look, Ma, no hands.'"

"We know things might go wrong. But the alternative could be much worse. You let us know when you and Mick are here and the guys have the roadblocks in place. Then we'll put the white paper in the window."

"And when he contacts you with the next instruction, we'll know he's seen the paper and must be nearby, and that's when we 'swoop,' as you say. Swooping is the part that sounds too simple."

"Oh ye of little faith. You have more than just me here. You've got a whole book club for backup."

"Just you and Brooke from the book club," Eileen said when Faith disconnected. "But Jan doesn't need to know that. Midge and I have reduced the search area. It's marshy in through there and not very built up."

"Knocking on doors, this time," Midge said. "Looking for a lost dog. We'll go now before the road is blocked."

"Are you sure?" Faith asked. "Because there's something we haven't considered. What if there's another accomplice staying with Gloria?"

"We'll be careful," Midge said.

"Very careful," Eileen said, "and we'll call when we find her."

After locking the door behind them, Faith turned to Brooke. "Is careful good enough?"

"It's what we've got. That, smarts, and the police."

Faith nodded. "Okay then. Phase two." She sent a text to their own accomplices—Rachel, Charlotte, and Alyssa: *Begin now. Report progress. THANK YOU.*

The call from Jan Rooney about the roadblocks came as soon as Faith had hit Send. Jan said that she and Mick Tobin were in position, watching the manor on opposite sides. Faith gave a nod to Brooke. Brooke taped the white paper in the window.

Rachel reported in first.

"Heath's at a window," Faith told Brooke. "Second floor, with binoculars trained on the cottage. And bingo! He must've seen the white paper. He's left the window. Rachel's texting Charlotte to be on the lookout."

"Where's Charlotte now?" Brooke asked.

"Waiting near Heath's room."

Charlotte's text came a few minutes later: *He returned to room.*

"He's going to make his move soon," Faith said. "But not by car, even without the roadblock. Alyssa just reported in. She's let the air out of his tires."

"Go, Alyssa!" Brooke cheered.

Then Eileen called and Faith could barely hear her over yapping in the background, but three words came through loud and clear. "We have her!"

The last call was a distorted voice telling Faith to listen carefully.

"Sorry, Heath," Faith said. "Wrong number."

"Sometimes simple is best," Faith said to Officer Rooney as they watched Officer Tobin putting Heath into the back of his vehicle.

"Sometimes we're lucky," Jan said. "Credit where credit's due, though. You did good work. Right down to the intersecting lines on your map. Of course, it helped that you had four days more than we did. And that Westcott is as much an amateur as all of you."

Faith considered saying, *We'll do even better next time*, but decided against it.

"Maybe I can get a book deal out of it," Heath said. "I know that's what Tanya was planning. She started going on about what a shame it was to waste a good crime. She would've put this in a book and someone would've seen through it. She was becoming a liability."

"He's his own liability," Faith whispered to Jan.

"No need to whisper. He can't hear us," Jan said. They were watching Officer Tobin and another officer interrogate Heath at the Lighthouse Bay Police Department. "Some guys like to sing as soon as you read them their rights. They're my favorite flavor of bad guy."

"It's kind of painful to hear," Faith said.

Heath said he was ambitious, Tanya was clever, and they both wanted more. They met when she signed books where he worked. "She called it my book graveyard," he said. Over coffee, they'd hatched their plot. Tanya already had her invitation to Simmering Suspense Week and wanted to write full time. Heath was familiar with Castleton Manor and Lighthouse Bay and dreamed of opening a bigger, better bookstore. The Jaxons had more money than they knew what to do with and had been able to realize their dream of owning a literary resort. He saw nothing wrong with getting them to help fund the dreams of the less fortunate—a bookstore they planned to call The Grim Reader.

"Greed's a nasty trait," Jan said to Faith. "The undoing of many budding criminal careers."

Heath went on to say that he had begun to worry about Tanya. She'd developed a theory about Jed's writing and odd similarities she said she'd found in some of Gloria's books. She became obsessed with Gloria and her fame.

Faith heard Mick ask Heath how he'd planned to get away with it.

"Because I'm smarter than Tanya. I made sure Gloria never saw me and would only be able to identify Tanya. It's possible Tanya thought we wouldn't let Gloria live, but that was never part of it. Gloria is a treasure. Tanya was expendable. She was under the impression we'd split the money. But that was mine. The necklace and book were for her."

"Have Mick ask him why he chose the box and access code he did," Faith said.

Jan communicated with Mick.

"The code is my lucky number—the birth date I share with the great Michael Patrick."

So I was right.

"Box three was for Tanya. Because in fairy tales you always get three wishes."

Gloria's Mary Stewart necklace and the Patrick *Grimm's Fairy Tales* were found in Heath's suitcase. Jan returned the book to Faith. After hearing Faith's worries about it, the officer agreed it would be safer back where it belonged than in the evidence locker. Jan returned the necklace to Gloria, who'd been found unharmed and had returned to Castleton Manor. Jan said that they had Heath's confession and knew where to find the book and necklace if they needed them.

A few hours later, Jed was released from custody. When he arrived back at the manor, he hardly left Gloria's side, and they revealed a long-held secret.

"I've never written a book in my life. Gloria writes them. I just play the part in public, since she hates it so much." Their partnership had started years before, when a woman's name on a thriller doomed it. "I can talk the talk after all these years of being the public face for the Jed Knowlan books. You want a writer's tips and tricks? I've got them. Do *I* write? I've tried, but I'm no good at stories."

"Is your name even Jed Knowlan?" Marlene asked.

He gave her a rueful grin. "Jim Norton. I own a small trucking business in Ohio."

"Are you a runner?" Brooke asked, one eyebrow raised.

At first he didn't seem inclined to answer.

"Tell them," Gloria said, swatting his arm. "They deserve to know and you need to stop hiding it."

"I've been playing around—"

"Writing," Gloria corrected.

"Poetry. But it isn't good enough for public consumption yet. I work at it when I'm out walking. Running is my cover story. See? I'm no good at stories."

Gloria surprised Faith and Marlene by telling them she was looking forward to her Friday afternoon interview. "With one change, if you don't mind. There's no need for an interviewer. I'll simply tell my story."

And she did, to a full house, wearing the glittering Mary Stewart necklace. Alyssa, Rachel, and Jed sat in the front row. Sir Arfer had his own chair next to Gloria.

"This is a story about what can happen when you only see what you want to," Gloria told her rapt audience. "We'll call the story 'Clueless at Castleton Manor.'"

Tanya had lured her away, telling her that Charlotte understood her need for privacy and had arranged for her to stay somewhere other than the manor full of adoring fans. She'd found a charming and secluded cottage, and someone would drive her to and from the resort each day. Touched by Charlotte's solicitude, Gloria wrote her a thank-you note, which must have been replaced by the ransom note. She'd been making tremendous progress on her new book and didn't question it when Tanya told her that Marlene had agreed to let her skip some of the Simmering Suspense programs.

"I still love fairy tales," Gloria said, "and the idea of dreams coming true. And I will admit I can also be an old fool."

During her time away, she never felt threatened, the fridge and pantry were full, and she was in the "writing zone." She was distraught when Sir Arfer chased Tanya out the front door that first morning, but he was a rascal that way and Tanya had brought him back. He had a nice fenced-in area behind the cottage and seemed to have made friends with a cat that showed up every so often. She thought she'd lost her phone. Afterward, she realized that Tanya had probably taken it. She was disappointed she had no Internet access, but otherwise she was in writing heaven.

"You might ask if I ever tried to leave the house. I am a firm believer in beautiful scenery—as long as it stays where it belongs, which is outside the window. So no, I was happy in my own world." She stopped and touched the short curls on her head. "I hadn't realized Tanya worked as a hair stylist in her day job. She was right. I feel absolutely liberated by my new short hair."

During refreshments after the program, Gloria apologized to Charlotte for her bad manners in faking illness at the opening reception, explaining that her nerves had gotten the better of her. She charmingly invited Alyssa to have tea with her. She greeted Rachel warmly and told her she'd been absolutely sick over the First Chapters Contest. She hadn't realized that as the judge, she would be required to sign a waiver assuring that she had no bias and must disqualify entries by relatives, associates, or friends. She'd recognized Rachel's entry immediately and had felt bound to disqualify it. She'd tried to contact Rachel to say she wanted to take the manuscript to her own agent.

"I didn't open your e-mails because I was so angry," Rachel said. "Would you really do that?"

"With the utmost pleasure."

Charlotte caught Faith as she was leaving the Great Hall Gallery after the program. "Wolfe called. He expects to be back for the dinner this evening. He said he'd like to speak with you. And I'd like you and the other members of the Candle House Book Club to be my guests this evening, although it doesn't begin to repay you."

"Thank you, Charlotte. There's no question of repayment. But I'm sure everyone will want to join us if they can."

22

The seven-course dinner re-created from Gloria's *Murder With a Twist of Strychnine* that came at the end of Simmering Suspense Week was a delicious success. Marlene complained again about the incorrect appetizers, but Brooke ignored her and made shrimp puffs in honor of Watson.

Eileen sat on one side of Faith, Charlotte across from her. The chair on Faith's other side was vacant. Brooke hadn't joined them for obvious reasons, and Midge was busy concocting her recipe for Red Herrings.

Eileen leaned close and spoke confidentially to Faith. "Charlotte and I have come up with a plan to help Lindsey's family. We're going to create a local fund to help families with the cost of daycare, thanks mostly to a very generous donation from Charlotte. Lindsey will be the first recipient."

"That's lovely," Faith said.

They were eating dessert when Faith saw Charlotte's face light up. Faith thought at first that it was because of the dessert—out-of-this-world chocolate flan. She had just taken a bite of it—a rather large bite—when she felt a light touch on her shoulder. She looked up and there was Wolfe. *Lovely. Caught with my mouth full again.*

"That looks good," he said, taking the seat next to her and reaching across the table to squeeze his mother's hand.

"It's fabulous," Faith and Charlotte both said.

A server hurried over to offer Wolfe any part of the meal he wanted. He declined and told Faith and Charlotte he'd just arrived from the airport and wasn't sure what time or day it was, or what meal he should be looking forward to. He let go of Charlotte's hand and looked from her to Faith.

"Mother called me on my return flight and filled me in."

"But not so you could sit there with that paternalistic glower," Charlotte said.

"You're terrible at reading faces, Mother. I'm not glowering. I'm thankful beyond belief that neither of you got hurt. And that isn't me being surprised or condescending, either. Frankly, I'm in awe. Faith, you did a remarkable job. I'm sorry my trip to London made things harder. But now I can show you why I went." He glanced around the room full of people deep in conversations and dessert. He nodded toward the door. "Come on out here."

Faith started to leave her dessert but thought better of it. The chocolate flan was too good to leave behind, so she brought it with her. She followed Wolfe into the grand marble entry hall. Whenever she saw Wolfe standing here, she tried to picture him as a seven-year-old bouncing through the front door. She imagined his small voice echoing off the vaulted ceiling as he called, "I'm home."

Adult Wolfe looked completely comfortable in the large space. He stopped at the base of the broad stairway. "I didn't want to take the chance of anyone else oohing and ahhing over this and passing it around." He pulled a small book-size parcel wrapped in tissue from the inside pocket of his jacket and handed it to her, taking her plate and napkin in exchange.

The size and shape of the package gave her pause at first, sending her mind back to the box with Gloria's braid. But this package wasn't brown and it definitely felt like a book, the size of a modern paperback, but heavier and more substantial. More exciting.

"Hang on a sec." She tucked the package under her arm, took her napkin back from him, and wiped her hands again to make sure there were no traces of flan. Then she handed the napkin back and removed the tissue.

Inside was a leather-bound book. In the center of the cover a small oval frame had been tooled. A ship sailed in the center of the frame, which was styled to look like a coil of rope. She turned the book to look at the spine and then the back cover. There was another tooled rope oval there, and in its center sat a cat.

"Here's your buddy," Wolfe said.

"Hmm?" Faith looked up.

Wolfe put her plate on a side table. Watson sat at the other end of the table.

Faith held the book up so that she saw Watson and the cat on the back cover side by side. "You look like a cover cat, Watson—handsome and heroic. Please behave yourself, though. Even heroes should have good manners."

"He might be wondering if you're ever going to open the book," Wolfe said.

Faith opened it and admired the endpapers—watercolors of ocean waves swirling with sea creatures. She read the title page aloud: "Sea Shanties of the Cape Cod Whalemen: An Illustrated Collection by Michael Patrick, Truro, Massachusetts, 1922."

"It's the only known copy," Wolfe said. "I'd heard rumors about its existence for years, and every so often I've sent out feelers to see if I could find it. A couple of months ago I heard it might be coming up for auction in London."

"And you went to bring it home."

"Close to home, anyway. If there were a Patrick museum in Truro, the book would belong there. But there isn't, so I knew it would receive the best care here at Castleton Manor."

"Thank you, Wolfe. This is an incredible gift for the library. Hey—" A puzzle piece slipped into place. "Do you ever do business with Corrie at The Fishwife's Attic?"

"Occasionally. Would you like to see my favorite song?" She handed him the book, and he carefully turned pages until he found what he was looking for.

"I don't think I've ever heard it," Faith said when he handed it back to her.

"You've never heard 'Cape Cod Girls'? Well, we need to fix that, at least with a few verses. But you'll have to pretend I'm dressed like one of Captain Angus Jaxon's deck crew."

"With or without a peg leg?"

"Peg leg optional, eye patch a must." Wolfe closed one eye, smiled, and started singing.

Faith decided Wolfe's gravelly baritone was well suited for sea shanties, and probably piratical eye patches as well. She followed along in Patrick's book, delighted by his illustrations for the verses about clever Cape Cod girls who had no combs but brushed their hair with codfish bones, and Cape Cod boys who had no sleds but slid down hills on codfish heads. The last verse, though—that was the best. The cat from the back appeared in three pen, ink, and watercolor sketches, and that cat—a tailless cat—proved to be every bit as clever as the Cape Cod girls and boys. The cat danced a hornpipe with the children, he rode on the back of a codfish, and he sat handsomely next to a soup bowl on someone's supper table looking just the least bit smug.

"It *is* Watson," Faith said when Wolfe finished singing the cat's verse. "Look." She showed Wolfe the illustrations.

"That's one of the reasons I thought you'd like the book as much as I do," he said. He sang a line from that verse again. *Cape Cod cats ain't got no tails. They lost them all in the northeast gales.*

"This proves Watson's a genuine Cape Cod cat now," he said when he finished. "And I hope it means that he and his human will stick around."

The cat appreciated fine music as much as the next clever feline, but he also believed in discretion, so he hadn't commented on the vocal quality of the human male's "song." Nor on the first several verses, even though the lyrics were improved by frequent mentions of codfish. But the words in the last verse—they might have been written about him. Had they been written about him? They must have been. He'd always known the feeble story of "an accident" when he was a kitten hadn't been the real story. And here was proof, immortalized in song, that he'd lost his tail bravely battling a northeast gale. And how appropriate that his human found the proof in one of those books she devoted most of her time to and loved almost as much as she loved him. How satisfying it was to know that although he didn't have much of a tail, he did have a hero's tale. Even more than music, the cat appreciated fine logic.

"Listen," Faith said to Wolfe. "I think Watson wants us to stick around too. He's purring."

Learn more about Annie's fiction books at

AnniesFiction.com

- Access your e-books
- Discover exciting new series
- Read sample chapters
- Watch video book trailers
- Share your feedback

We've designed the Annie's Fiction website especially for you!

Plus, manage your account online!

- Check your account status
- Make payments online
- Update your address

Visit us at AnniesFiction.com